The Murdered Mermaid

APRIL FERNSBY

DEDICATION

For Rosie and Eve.

Chapter 1

"So, let's recap," I said to Oliver and Stanley across the kitchen table. "Any one of the residents in Brimstone could be plotting a murder at this very moment. We don't know who, and we don't know where."

Stanley, my cat and familiar, nodded. "That's right so far. That nasty, evil, malicious Astrid said she'd been secretly changing the memories of residents so that they'll now have thoughts of murder racing through their minds." He waved his paw angrily in the air. "I wish I could get my paws on her!"

Oliver, his brother, said calmly, "What's done is done. We have to deal with the fallout of what Astrid did. Carry on, Cassia, what was your next point?"

I continued, "As a justice witch in the town, it's my duty to deal with any crimes, including murders. Blythe and Gran are supposed to help me. But they're missing in action, thanks to Astrid and her devious plan. The guardians of the town can help me with any investigation, but the one in charge, Luca, doesn't remember me and looked at me with hate when we last met. Again, thanks to Astrid." I picked up my cup of tea and took a drink.

Oliver said, "And? We know all of this. Cassia, what's your point?"

I shrugged. "I was seeing how bad our situation is. I don't think it can get much worse."

Stanley groaned, rolled off the chair and landed on the floor. "You've cursed us now. Things are going to get a lot, lot worse. In ways that we can't even imagine." He groaned again for good measure and rested his head on his paws.

"Stanley!" Oliver admonished. "There's no need to be so dramatic. Yes, things look bleak at the moment and Cassia won't be able to trust a soul in Brimstone, but it's not the end of the world."

1

Stanley looked up at his brother. "It feels like it. Luca doesn't remember me either. We were friends; good friends." He shook his head sadly. "And now Cassia's too scared to go back into Brimstone. The residents have probably killed each other by now."

I bristled. "I am not too scared to go back! I'm just taking a day or two to gather my thoughts."

Oliver gave me a stern look. "You don't have that many thoughts in your head, young lady. Have you come up with a plan of action yet? You can't sit here all day drinking tea and hoping the problems in Brimstone will go away on their own. You're a justice witch, the only one at the moment, and it's your duty to deal with whatever is going on in Brimstone."

I put my cup down. "I know that. It's just that…" I trailed off. I had no excuses. I knew I should go back to Brimstone and deal with the aftermath of what Astrid had done.

Astrid had been a guardian in the magical town of Brimstone. She was also the girlfriend of my childhood friend, Luca. She had hated me on first sight and had let her feelings be known. She had hindered my murder investigations a few times and had caused serious problems with the last one I'd dealt with. She'd stolen a magical potion called Memory Mist which had the ability to change someone's memories and how they would act in the future. Astrid boasted that she'd whispered murderous thoughts into many a residents' ear. The result would be more murders in Brimstone. She'd also removed all memories of Stanley and me from Luca's mind. I tried not to think about how coldly Luca had looked at me when Astrid had done that. That last part had happened yesterday, and I'd immediately returned to Gran's house to metaphorically lick my wounds. And drink lots of tea.

Oliver sighed impatiently. "Cassia! Come out of your daydream. You need to get back to Brimstone immediately and face up to your responsibilities! What will Esther and

2

Blythe say when they come back and find the town in chaos and realise that you've done nothing to help?"

"Okay, you don't have to shout."

Oliver shouted, "I think I do! Someone has to! Are you a brave Winter witch or a scared little mouse?"

"I'm a brave Winter witch," I mumbled. I looked away from his accusing eyes.

"Pardon? Was that the mumbling of a tiny mouse?" Oliver put his paw to the side of his ear. Who was being dramatic now?

I slammed my hand on the table and declared, "I'm a brave Winter witch! I'm going back to Brimstone right now! I'm going to face danger head-on!"

Oliver said, "There's no need to shout. I'm not deaf."

Stanley called out from his prone position on the floor, "Quiet! I can hear a noise in the cellar. I think someone's knocking at the door."

We all remained silent as Stanley concentrated on the noise. My heart missed a beat at the thought of someone knocking on the cellar door below us. The cellar door led to Brimstone. Despite me telling Gran many times to put a lock on the door, she'd refused. Which meant that if someone was now knocking on the door, they could easily come through and into Gran's house.

Stanley hissed, "There is definitely someone knocking at the door!"

I went over to Stanley's side and crouched next to him. "Is it an angry knock? Is it the knock of a mad creature who's murdered everyone in Brimstone and is now after us?"

Stanley listened again. "It's quite a polite knock. There it is again. Whoever it is isn't going away until you answer the door." He got to his paws and said, "I'll go and see who it is. You wait here."

I looked at my grey-haired friend and smiled at him. "Thank you, but I'll open the door."

Stanley held a paw up. "No, I insist. I'd rather put myself in danger. It's my duty to look after you."

I shook my head. "No. I'm the witch. I know how to do magic. It's best that I go."

Oliver jumped down from his chair and let out an angry hiss. "You two are testing my patience! I'll go!"

He padded quickly away with his tail in the air twitching angrily.

We went after him. He was nimble on his paws and was downstairs and standing at the cellar door before we caught up with him. Without any warning, Oliver popped his head through the cat flap.

"Oliver!" Stanley cried out. "Don't get your head chopped off!"

Oliver's head came back, thankfully still attached to his body. He said quietly, "It's Luca. He doesn't look happy." He padded over to my side.

I slowly opened the cellar door and looked out at my friend with a small smile on my face.

My smile froze when I saw the hate in Luca's eyes as he glowered at me. I'd never seen him look like that at anyone. What had Astrid said to him to make him stare at me like that?

Luca thrust my broomstick towards me and said coldly, "You left this in Blythe's house yesterday."

I took my broomstick and said, "Has Blythe returned?"

"No." Luca made to turn away.

I went on, "Have you heard anything from her?"

Luca looked me over before replying. "Not that it's any of your business, but no, I haven't. This is a polite warning; keep away from Brimstone. I don't know who you are but I don't trust you. If I find you in Brimstone, I will arrest you and detain you in a cell until Blythe returns."

I heard Stanley gasp in shock at my side. He suddenly leapt into Luca's arms. Luca had no choice but to hold him. My heart twisted at the disgusted look Luca gave Stanley.

Stanley put a paw on either side of Luca's face and said, "Luca, don't you remember us? Don't you remember me? We're friends. We used to play together when you were little. You've helped Cassia and me with our investigations. You must remember. You must!"

Luca roughly placed Stanley on the ground and snapped, "Don't ever do that to me again! You could have fleas."

Stanley's head dropped and he took a step back. He mumbled, "I'm sorry."

Something snapped inside me. No one was going to talk to Stanley like that!

I waved my broomstick in the air and said to Luca, "Don't you ever, ever talk to Stanley like that again! I don't know what Astrid's done to you, but you will not take it out on Stanley or me!"

Luca folded his arms. "Astrid? What do you know about Astrid?"

"More than I want to! She's messed with your memories."

He snorted in derision. "She would never do that to me. Astrid is the love of my life."

"Yeah? Where is she now?" I demanded. I looked over Luca's shoulder to make sure Astrid wasn't standing behind him with a sneaky look on her face. She had a habit of doing that.

Luca said, "She's gone away for a while on important business." He frowned. "I think that's what she told me."

"Pah!" I waved my broomstick in the air. "She's told you a pack of lies. She's been lying to everyone in Brimstone."

"She has," Stanley added meekly.

Luca unfolded his arms and jabbed a finger in my direction. "That's a lie! You're the liar. You're the one who's caused problems in Brimstone and I won't allow you back in." He reached for the handle on the cellar door.

I was fuming with rage now and I bashed him on the hand with the bushy end of my broomstick. He yelped in surprise and pulled his hand back.

I raised my broomstick in warning. My voice was steady as I said, "You will not tell me what to do, Luca. You are a guardian in Brimstone, but I am a justice witch. I am your superior whether you remember me or not. Thanks to your girlfriend, there are problems brewing in Brimstone, and I'm going to be the one who deals with them." I took a step forward. "And you can't stop me. Understand?"

Luca rubbed his hand. He looked as if he were going to say something but then abruptly turned on his heel and walked away.

Stanley said proudly, "Cassia, that was awesome. You really put him in his place."

I lowered my broomstick. "I wish I hadn't hit him. I don't know what came over me."

Oliver said, "It was only a tap on his hand. He'll get over it. Perhaps you should whack him on the head and try to knock some sense into him." He paused and added. "You did well, Cassia. You stood up for yourself."

Wow. Getting praise from Oliver was a rare occurrence. It boosted my ego and made me declare, "Come on, Stanley, let's return to Brimstone. We've got work to do. Oliver, are you coming with us?"

"No, I'll stay here in case your gran comes back." There was worry in his voice. "I'm sure Esther will come back soon. She has to."

I gave him a nod. "Okay. We'll stay in touch with you."

I stepped through the cellar door. Stanley was right behind me.

Chapter 2

We paused and looked out onto the lovely town of
Brimstone. A white gazebo held a central position in the
large square of grass right in the middle of the town.
Benches and picnic tables were placed around it and they
were occupied by the smiling residents of Brimstone.
Brightly coloured buildings were arranged around the
square and many supernatural creatures strolled happily
along the pavement.

Stanley said, "It doesn't look like anyone's been
murdered."

"Not yet," I added. "I think we should pay a visit to Brin
and see what's been happening since we left here yesterday
in such a rush."

We walked along the cobbled path in front of us and
paused when we came to a tree covered in yellow and
green Brimstone butterflies. I smiled up at them. There
was a flutter of wings which sent a warm breeze my way.

Stanley laughed. "It's like they're saying hello and giving
us a hug. I love the Brimstone butterflies." He waved at
them. "Hello!"

We made our way to the large house that Blythe
occupied. She was a three-hundred-year-old witch who
ruled Brimstone. Or she had until she'd gone off
gallivanting somewhere with Gran. They'd left notes
before they'd left informing us not to worry about them.
Of course we were going to worry! I tutted to myself as I
thought how irresponsible they'd been.

Stanley must have heard my tut as he trotted at my side
because he said, "Are you thinking about Blythe and
Esther again?"

I nodded.

Stanley continued, "You shouldn't be mad with them.
You know it was Astrid's fault that they left so abruptly.

They are powerful witches. They can look after themselves."

I sighed. "I suppose so. But that doesn't stop me worrying about them."

We walked along the sparkling path that led to Blythe's front door. Brin opened it before we reached the door.

Brin was a house brownie who worked with Blythe. She knew everything that went on in this town and I was counting on her to help us.

Brin was wearing her usual attire of a white apron over a brown dress. She flapped a duster at us as we approached and said, "I've been cleaning this house non-stop since you left yesterday. Cleaning usually helps to soothe my mind, but it's not working today. Have you heard anything from Esther?" She opened the door wider and we stepped inside.

I shook my head. "I gather you haven't heard anything from Blythe?"

Brin shoved her duster in her apron pocket. "I haven't." She closed the door behind us and led us through to the living room. She indicated for us to take a seat.

Once we were settled on the sofa, Brin pulled a small chair closer to us, sat down and gave us an intense look. She said, "I had a strange conversation with Luca yesterday. He claims he doesn't know you. Tell me exactly what Astrid did to him."

I smiled at her. "How did you know Astrid did anything to him?"

"Who else would be evil enough to do such a thing?"

I told Brin about my last encounter with Astrid and how she'd boasted about the destruction she'd left in her wake.

Brin's lips tightened in annoyance. When I'd finished, she said, "Oh! That evil being! She'll get her comeuppance! Somehow."

I twisted my hands together and asked, "I was wondering if there was something I could do to help Luca. Could I use magic on him to restore his memories? If there's going to be a spate of murders in Brimstone, I could do with his help."

Brin shook her head. "We can't take that chance. Astrid may have cast an extra spell on him and if you use magic on his mind, it could wipe out all of his memories. He wouldn't even know his name. There is a chance that his memories of you and Stanley might return on their own." She gave me a small smile. "You'll just have to win him over with your lovely personality."

Stanley sniffed and said sadly, "He threw me to the floor and said I might have fleas. I've never had fleas in my life."

I picked Stanley up and placed him on my knee. I stroked his little head and said, "Luca's not himself. You know that. Once he gets to know you again, he'll see how special you are."

"I hope so." Stanley put his head on my arm.

Brin looked towards the big window that overlooked the town. She said, "I haven't noticed anyone acting out of character this morning. But there again, they could be walking around with murder in their minds but with smiles on their faces. There's not much we can do about that. What a horrible situation this is."

"I know. I feel so helpless. Is there anything I can do? Should I talk to the residents and see if Astrid spoke to anyone recently?"

Brin shook her head. "I saw Astrid talking to many beings recently when she was supposedly helping you with your last murder enquiry." She turned away from the window. "There is something you can do. I've been informed of suspicious behaviour in an area of Brimstone. I'd like you to investigate that area and see what you think. It could be nothing, but it's better to nip these things in the bud."

"Of course I'll investigate. Which area are we talking about? The forest? The mountains?"

"The beach," Brin said.

Stanley raised his head. "The beach? Brimstone has a beach? Where? Cassia, did you know Brimstone had a beach?"

"I didn't." I looked out of the window as if expecting sand dunes to appear next to the gazebo. "Where is it?"

"About ten miles away over the fields to the west. You have been there before, Cassia, with your mum." She stopped talking and colour came to her cheeks. Mum's name wasn't mentioned often in Brimstone.

I shifted in my seat and Stanley shifted on my knee. I suspected he was as uncomfortable as me about Mum being mentioned. Astrid had left us with a parting gift about information concerning Mum.

I cleared my throat nervously and said to Brin, "Astrid told me something about Mum yesterday. I don't know if I believe her, but I can't stop thinking about what she said."

Brin looked at me without blinking. "What did she tell you?"

"She said Luca was responsible for Mum's death, and that everyone in Brimstone knows that. Except me, of course."

"And me," Stanley added. "Everyone's been keeping it a secret from us." He looked at me with sad eyes. "We feel betrayed, don't we?"

My eyes began to sting and my vision blurred. I stroked Stanley's head again and gave him a small nod.

Brin reached out and put her little hand on my arm. In a gentle tone, she said, "Part of what Astrid told you is true. The town does know how your mum died. Blythe told us not to talk to you about it until she'd spoken to you. But it's been one murder after another recently and she hasn't had the time to have that conversation with you."

My stomach clenched in anger. "But Gran knew! She could have told me! Everyone's been lying to me. Why?"

"It was Blythe's orders. She said it was the right thing to do. Esther disagreed with her, but Blythe convinced her to be patient." She squeezed my arm. "I'm sorry if it's hard for you to accept, Cassia, but Blythe thought she was doing the right thing."

I shrugged. "I'm not sure about that. Was it Luca's fault that Mum died? What did he do?"

Brin pulled her hand back. "He didn't do anything apart from getting lost in the forest one day. Like yourself, he was only seven when your mum died. He'd only just discovered his shapeshifting abilities and he was in his rabbit form when he got himself into trouble. Your mum rescued him by putting herself in danger." Brin's eyes welled up. "I don't know the full details, but I do know it was a terrible accident. Your mum saved Luca's life but lost her own by doing so."

Tears escaped from my eyes. "Does Luca know what happened? He's never spoken to me about it."

Brin nodded. "When the accident happened, he was distraught and wouldn't stop screaming. Blythe used a spell to take his memory of the accident away. It was for the best. It wasn't his fault that your mum died and Blythe didn't want him carrying that guilt around."

"But he must have known. Astrid talked about Mum's death in front of him."

Brin's hands curled into little fists. "Astrid must have told him. But what exactly did she tell him? Did she make out it was his fault? Just when I thought she'd done her worst! I'll have to talk to Luca and see what she said to him. Don't you worry about this; I'll deal with Luca." She gave me a sad smile. "I'm sorry about your mum. I'll talk to Blythe when she returns and make sure she explains everything to you. Your mum's death was an accident; a terrible accident."

I brushed my tears away. "I don't want to talk about Mum anymore. Tell me more about this beach that I can't remember."

There was a flash of green light and someone appeared in the room.

Brin turned to the visitor and said, "At last! I thought you'd never get here."

Chapter 3

I looked at the man who had appeared in the room. He was slim and seemed to be about my height. I'd put his age at early to mid-twenties. His short brown hair stuck up in spikes and I caught flecks of green mixed in with the brown. He was wearing light green trousers and a plain, white shirt. A waistcoat was fastened over his shirt which had leaves and butterflies embroidered on it. His friendly face was turned my way and his light green eyes twinkled as if he'd just been told the best joke ever.

He clasped his hands together and jigged from foot to foot. He burst out, "Cassia Winter! I'm so excited to be here!"

Brin stood up and walked over to the excited man. She held her arms out and the young man lowered himself and then hugged her warmly. "Brin! So very good to see you again."

Brin took a step back and said, "Jeremy, you haven't aged a day since I last saw you. How much magic are you using on your looks?"

Jeremy laughed. "What's the point of being a witch if I can't use magic on myself?"

He was a witch? I shared a confused look with Stanley.

Jeremy laughed again at our befuddled expressions and moved closer to us. He perched himself on the small chair that Brin had vacated and gave us the warmest of smiles. The twinkle in his eyes increased and I noticed flecks of gold in them.

He held his hand out. "I'm Jeremy Spring. I'm a witch. One of the season witches just like you, Cassia Winter."

I took his hand. It was warm and after I shook it, I didn't let go. I said, "I've never met another witch. Apart from my gran and Blythe, of course. I only found out recently about the witches who are named after seasons."

Jeremy left his hand in mine and continued to smile at me. "I know all about you. I've been friends with Blythe and Esther for years." His smile dropped slightly. "I knew your mum too. Rosalyn and I worked together many times. I was sorry to hear of her passing. You have her same eyes." He removed his hand from mine and gently touched the end of my nose. "And the very same freckle on the end of your nose. I hope you don't mind me talking about Rosalyn."

I smiled at the charming witch in front of me. "I don't mind at all." I hesitated. "In fact, I would like to hear more about her."

"And I would be delighted to tell you." Jeremy turned his attention to Stanley. "I've heard about you too, Stanley. I know how much you've helped Cassia, and how brave you are. You're a handsome-looking cat. Has anyone ever told you that?"

Stanley let out a little cat chuckle. "It has been mentioned once or twice. Do you know my brother, Oliver?"

Jeremy nodded. "I do. I've had a few conversations with him." He moved his head closer and said, "Is he still bossy?"

I nodded on Stanley's behalf.

Brin came over to us with a tray of tea things. I hadn't even noticed her leaving the room. She placed the items on a table at my side and said, "I hope coffee is okay with everyone. Cassia, Jeremy is here to help you with your next investigation. I hope that's okay with you?"

I gave Brin a wary look. "Why do I need help?"

Jeremy said, "It was my idea to offer my services. I keep an eye on Brimstone Beach and have done for years. I used to help your mum when any problems arose there. I know the beach well, and the beings who live there. I was on patrol there a few days ago when I felt a change in the air." He frowned as he considered his next words. "I can't quite explain it. It's like there's an expectation of evil in the air. As if the area is waiting for something terrible to happen. Do you know what I mean?"

"I do." I took the cup that Brin passed my way and said thank you to her. "We've experienced that same feeling a lot in Brimstone recently. Do you know about the black magic that was forced into our town?"

Jeremy gave me a grim smile. "I do. All the season witches know about it. I also know that Blythe and Esther have left Brimstone and gone after Blythe's cousins as she thinks they're responsible for the black magic."

My cup shook in my hands. "Have you heard anything about them? Are they okay?"

"They will be. They're not alone." Jeremy took a sip of his coffee. "The other season witches are on their way to help Blythe and Esther as we speak. They'll be back home before you know it." He shot me a reassuring smile. "In the meantime, I'd like to help you with the possible trouble at Brimstone Beach. When you had your problem with the black magic here, some of it made its way to the beach. I was hoping it wouldn't affect anyone there, but it seems I may be wrong. We can head that way after our lovely coffee and I'll explain everything on the journey. If that's okay with you, Cassia? I don't want to get in your way."

There was a reassuring presence about Jeremy and I felt instinctively that I could trust him. I looked down at Stanley and said, "What do you think?"

Stanley turned his little head towards Jeremy and said, "I would like that. I'm getting a good feeling from you. You smell good too. Like new leaves on a tree."

Jeremy grinned. "I like you too, Stanley. If we have time, will you show me around Brimstone? I haven't been here for years and I'd love to have a nosy around it. Do all the supernatural creatures still get along with each other?"

"Mostly," I told him. "I've dealt with five murders recently, and I was hoping there wouldn't be any more. But there could be. Jeremy, where do you live? Where have you come from? What kind of butterflies are those on your waistcoat?" I nodded in the direction of the creatures embroidered there. They had black wings with red bands along the outside of the wings. White spots adorned the top of the wings.

Jeremy laughed again. He did that a lot and I liked it. He said, "These are Red Admirals. And that's the town where I live. It's not quite as pretty as Brimstone, but it's home. We have the same supernatural creatures that you have here, but they don't live in harmony like yours do. The werewolves and vampires can't even bear to be on the same side of the street as each other. I'd invite you to come over for a visit but I'm afraid you'd be called in to settle a fight as soon as you stepped over the border into our town."

We chatted a bit more about the work Jeremy did in Red Admiral and I told him briefly about the murders in Brimstone. Jeremy was greatly saddened to hear about them. Stanley told him about Astrid and Luca. Jeremy lost his smile altogether and the twinkle in his eyes dimmed.

I said brightly, "Apart from the murders, Brimstone is a lovely place to be. We'll show you around later." I drained the last of my coffee and put my cup down. "Shall we head over to the beach now? I've got my broomstick with me. You could squeeze on it with me if you like?"

Jeremy put his cup down and clicked his fingers. A broom appeared in the air next to him. It was made of light green wood and had daffodils and tulips placed in the green bristles at the end of it. It looked like a work of art.

"Wow!" Stanley exclaimed. "Has your broomstick been here all this time? How did you make it appear? Can you show Cassia how to do that?"

Jeremy laughed and the twinkle came back into his eyes. "You have as many questions as Cassia. Let's head off now and I'll try to answer as many questions as I can on the way."

I looked over at Brin and said, "Will you be alright if we go? What if something happens here? What if the residents start turning on each other?"

Brin cast me a grim smile. "If that happens, I'll use an immobilising spell on the whole town and then I'll send you a message. I'm sure everything will be alright here, Cassia. You go to the beach with Jeremy. I've got a strong feeling that you're needed there."

Chapter 4

I was reluctant to leave Brin on her own but she insisted she'd be fine. I told her to contact me immediately if there was any trouble in Brimstone. Her smile was overly bright as she bid us farewell.

Stanley had given me a hopeful look as we stood on the path outside Blythe's house with Jeremy. He'd barely taken his attention off Jeremy's wonderful broomstick since the second it had appeared, so I knew what his hopeful look meant. That cat of mine loved flying and he'd already travelled on Blythe's broomstick as well as mine. I could see how eager he was to try out Jeremy's broomstick. He reminded me of one of those roller coaster addicts who travel the world looking for their next adrenalin rush.

I sent Stanley an understanding smile before saying to Jeremy, "Would you mind if Stanley flew with you? He loves going on different broomsticks and I can see how impressed he is with yours."

Stanley turned his little face towards Jeremy, his eyes wide with hope.

Jeremy gave him a broad smile. "I would love that! Stanley, hop aboard." He lowered his broomstick and Stanley was on it in a second.

I settled on my broomstick and followed Jeremy as he rose away from the path and over Brimstone town.

Jeremy turned his broomstick to the west and said, "The beach is about ten miles that way. I'll tell you about it as we fly along."

I stayed close to Jeremy's side as we made our way over fields and mountains.

He began, "The beach is five miles long. The area of sea that belongs to Brimstone stretches out for hundreds of miles. It's inhabited by the usual sea creatures that you'd expect to find."

"Like dolphins, whales and sharks?" I asked.

"Yes. And vampire squids, harpies, sirens, sea hags." He paused. "There are the mischievous grindylows, of course. You must watch out for them. They love dragging their victims into the sea."

I said, "What do the grindylows look like? I don't like the sound of them."

Jeremy gave me a warning look. "They're small and green. They often disguise themselves to look like seaweed. I'll watch out for them and warn you if I see any." He reached forward and stroked Stanley's head. "You keep well away from them, my little friend."

Keeping his head forward on the view, Stanley replied, "I'm not going anywhere near the sea. I don't like it. It's too wet."

Jeremy laughed. "You're right about that. Of course, the majority of the creatures who live in the sea are merpeople."

My broomstick wobbled. "Merpeople? Like mermaids and mermen?"

"Yes, of course." Jeremy looked my way. "Why do you look so shocked?"

"I just wasn't expecting to ever meet such creatures." A smile stretched across my face. "Wow. Merpeople. How exciting! What are they like?"

"Like everyone else." Jeremy hesitated before continuing. "Cassia, your mum used to spend a lot of time at the beach with the merpeople. Some of them might talk to you about her. Would that be alright? I could warn them not to if you prefer?"

"I honestly don't mind. I'm not sure what's come over me today, but I feel ready to talk about Mum. Did you work with Mum at the beach?"

Jeremy nodded. "We had many adventures together. There's a kraken who lives on the bottom of the seabed and he loves causing fights whenever there's a full moon! I think he's got a touch of the werewolf in him. Your mum and I had our hands full with the chaos he caused."

Jeremy went into more details as we flew along. His stories about Mum made my heart feel light and happy. It was clear that he'd been fond of her and had a great deal of respect for her. I felt like I was getting to know Mum for the first time.

Jeremy had just finished telling me a story about a drunken harpy when I spotted a line of blue on the horizon.

Stanley saw it too and yelled, "I can see the sea! Look! It's over there." He quickly stood up on his hind legs and waved his front paws in the air. "I can see the sea!"

Jeremy reached out and put a steadying hand on Stanley. "Whoa there! Be careful. You nearly fell off."

I shook my head at Stanley. Perhaps I should get him a broomstick seat with straps on it; the sort of thing that you'd use for an excited child. Maybe I should magic one up for him.

Jeremy headed towards the blue line. I was thankful to see he kept one hand on Stanley who was now sitting down again.

As we got closer to the sea, I could hear the sound of people chatting and laughing. Someone was singing and there was a faint twang of a guitar. We headed ever closer and the expanse of blue increased. The sun was shining on the sea and spots of sunlight danced like stars across the surface. I spotted a lighthouse perched on a cliff to our left. It was painted in the colours of the Brimstone butterflies: light green and yellow. Jeremy was saying something but I couldn't quite catch his words.

The sound of chatting increased and it was now mixed with the occasional cheer and yell. We reached the beach and I looked down at the wide expanse of golden sand. I saw a colourful array of beach chairs and towels strewn across the sand with people lounging on them. Tables were placed intermittently amongst them loaded with plates and cups. Nets and makeshift goals were dotted around the sand and people were playing games and yelling happily at each other. An open café made of wood was at the side of the beach, and the delicious smell of hot dogs, burgers and chips wafted towards us.

When I say people, I'm not sure they were human. The creatures playing and lounging on the beach looked human, but they were impressive specimens. Even from up high I could see how perfect they all looked with their toned bodies and beautiful faces. The sun caught the light glitter on their skin and highlighted every muscle and firm limb. Every creature was wearing skimpy beach clothes which didn't leave much to the imagination. Mind you, if I looked like that, I'd be dressed skimpily too.

Jeremy said, "I know; they're perfect, aren't they? It's like arriving at a photo shoot where only the most beautiful and ideal creatures are allowed. Those are the merpeople."

I couldn't stop staring at them as we came in for a landing. They were mesmerizing as they played ball games, lounged on the towels and delicately ate slices of fruit. One of them must have a spot. Surely? Or a small roll of fat somewhere? Was that too much to ask?

Some of them looked our way and gave us cheerful waves as we landed on the sand. I heard Jeremy's name called out in welcome. He raised a hand and smiled in response.

Stanley leapt off Jeremy's broomstick and landed on the sand. He sniffed it suspiciously and said, "It smells weird. I don't like it." He put his paw on something and rolled it to one side. "What is this?"

Jeremy laughed. "It's a shell. It used to have a sea creature in it."

Stanley's face creased in repulsion. "That's disgusting. What's it doing here on the sand? It should be back in the sea where it belongs."

Jeremy knelt at his side. "Haven't you been to the beach before?"

Stanley shook his head. "I haven't, and I don't think much about it so far. Does this sand stuff go on forever?

Where are the trees and flowers? And what's with the sea and that noise it's making? Can't someone switch it off?" He tutted as he glowered at the sea.

I took in the merpeople as they continued with their activities. "Jeremy, where are their tails? How are they able to walk around on legs? Does it hurt them?"

"No. The Brimstone merpeople have magical abilities which were bestowed on them by ancestors of yours. When they're in the sea, they have a tail. When they're on the beach, they have legs. It's that simple. As long as they don't stray too far from this area, they won't experience pain in their legs. If they do stray, they'll get shooting pains on the soles of their feet which then travels up their legs."

"What happens if they stay away from this area too long?" I asked.

"That's never happened. The merpeople know this is a safe place for them. A few foolish youngsters have wandered too far from this beach in the past. They experienced painful tingles in their limbs which was enough to send them racing back to the beach."

I persisted, "But what would happen if they went too far?"

Jeremy gave me a quizzical look. "I imagine they would experience an extreme amount of pain. It could even be fatal. Why are you asking me that?"

"I was thinking about what you said earlier about there being a change in the atmosphere here." I gave him a small smile. "I was thinking about how a merperson could be hurt by someone. Sorry. That's my murderous mind warming up. Since becoming a justice witch, I've started to think like a murderer. I hope that doesn't make me sound weird. I'm not planning on committing a murder. Honestly."

Jeremy gave me a warm smile. "I know what you mean. Why don't we go for an ice cream at the café over there? It's the best ice cream in the whole of Brimstone. I can tell you more about the merpeople and how things have changed recently."

"That's an excellent idea. What do you say, Stanley?" I looked down at the sand. My little friend wasn't there. "Stanley? Jeremy, where did Stanley go?"

A sudden anguished cry shot through the air. My blood ran cold. I knew that cry. It was Stanley's.

The cry came out again and I heard Stanley shout, "Cassia! Help!"

I looked towards where the noise was coming from. Stanley was at the edge of the sea. Long strips of dark, green seaweed were wrapped around his back legs.

Jeremy dropped his broomstick. "The grindylows! They've got Stanley!" He raced across the sand.

I couldn't move. I watched in shock as my beloved cat was dragged into the sea.

Chapter 5

Jeremy rushed across the sand calling out Stanley's name. The merpeople nearest to him stopped what they were doing and stared his way. Some began to run after him.

After a few frozen seconds, my senses returned to me and I dashed after Jeremy. I screamed, "Stanley! Come back!"

My feet pounded across the sand and my heart thudded in my chest. Stanley had completely disappeared beneath the waves.

Jeremy ran into the water and prepared to dive in. He suddenly stopped as a creature ascended from the water with a bedraggled Stanley in her arms. She looked at Jeremy and said something. I couldn't hear what she was saying because my heart was thudding like a drum in my ears. I ran into the water and over to Stanley. He leapt into my arms and I pulled his soggy body next to my chest. His little heart was beating as fast as mine. I closed my eyes and pulled him closer.

A female voice declared loudly, "Does this thing belong to you? What was it doing in my sea? Who let it in? As if I haven't got enough to do around here! Well? I'm waiting for an answer."

I registered a silence and realised the angry voice was directed my way. I opened my eyes and looked at the creature in front of me. Her skin sparkled and she was impossibly beautiful so I assumed she was a mermaid. She didn't have long, thick hair like the others; hers was short and spiky. There was a small tiara stuck amongst the spikes. Her blue eyes looked at me coolly.

I said, "Thank you for rescuing Stanley. I didn't know he was so close to the sea. I'm so sorry." My voice caught in my throat. "I thought he'd drowned. Thank you for bringing him back."

Stanley shivered in arms and muttered a shaky, "Thank you."

The mermaid's expression softened and she gave us a smile. "Stanley? Then you must be Cassia. I knew your mum. I was sorry to hear about her." She moved closer and placed a gentle hand on Stanley's wet head. "Are you okay? You have to be careful near the water's edge. Those grindylows are always on the lookout for something smaller than them to drag into the sea. They didn't mean you any harm. They wanted to play with you. I'll tell them to leave you alone."

Stanley continued to shiver in my arms. He attempted to talk, but his teeth were chattering too much.

I thought about the magic spells I'd been reading about recently and the perfect one came to my mind. I put Stanley on the sand and sat at his side. I pictured a giant hairdryer and felt magic travelling into my hands. I aimed them at Stanley and felt tingles in my fingers. A warm current of air flowed from my fingertips and over Stanley. His grey fur ruffled under the hot breeze coming from me. He moved his head left and right in the current and he started to purr. I smiled at his cute face and continued to focus on getting him dry.

When he was dry, he let out a little chuckle and said, "That was lovely. I'm tempted to run into the sea so you can do that again."

"Don't you dare," I told him. I picked him up and got to my feet.

Jeremy's eyes were welling with tears. He said, "You looked just like your mum then. She was always quick to perform spells to help others."

I smiled at him. "Don't be getting all soft on me." I turned my attention to the mermaid in front of me and noticed her eyes glistening too. I said, "I'm sorry, I don't know your name. I didn't even know this beach existed until a short while ago. I'm not familiar with who lives here."

The mermaid gave me a soft smile. "We've met before. You used to come here with your mum. I often saw you making sandcastles with Rosalyn. I used to bring you sparkling shells from the bottom of the sea. I'm Nerita."

"Hello, Nerita," Stanley said. "Pleased to meet you."

I looked at Nerita's tiara and said, "Are you a princess?"

Nerita laughed. "Sort of. My father, King Taron, rules this stretch of sea. He doesn't like coming onto the beach and says it isn't natural for merpeople to have legs. I look out for our people when they are up here as well as taking care of matters under the sea. Father isn't as strong as he used to be and there's a lot of work to be done at the moment." She abruptly stopped. "You don't want to hear about my problems. Pardon my nosiness, but why are you here, Cassia? Are you here for a friendly visit or is it work related? I know about your work as a justice witch in town."

Jeremy spoke for me, "I wanted Cassia to see where her mum worked. That's all. We're here for fun, not work." He gave Nerita a big smile.

Nerita gave him a suspicious look. "Are you sure about that? Jeremy, you know that I can deal with any issues with my people. I trust you won't interfere in any problems that may or may not arise."

"I wouldn't dream of it," Jeremy replied in a friendly manner. "I'm taking Cassia and Stanley to the café now. Perhaps we'll catch up with you later. Bye for now."

He put his hand on my arm and turned us away. I shot a smile at Nerita before being led firmly along the beach.

I whispered to Jeremy, "Why did you lie to her? If there's something funny going on here, she might know what it is."

Jeremy whispered back, "I think Nerita is behind the funny business. I'll explain everything in a minute. Where did we leave our broomsticks? Don't tell me those cheeky grindylows have pinched them."

"Are you looking for these?" A merman was standing a short distance ahead of us with Jeremy's broomstick in one hand and mine in the other. He held them towards us. "I saw what happened to your cat. Is he okay?"

We walked closer and retrieved our broomsticks. I kept Stanley in one arm. There was no way I was letting him go.

Jeremy said, "Hi, Conway. Yes, Stanley is okay, thank you. Your sister rescued him. This is Cassia."

Conway smiled at me. Just like everyone else, he was incredibly handsome. His short, spiky hair matched his sister's.

Conway said, "I hope Nerita didn't give you a hard time. She's been in a terrible mood these last few days and she's taking it out on anyone who gets too close to her."

"She was fine," I replied. "Why is she in a bad mood?"

Conway looked towards the sea before saying, "Because of the sirens. Jeremy, don't you know about them?"

Jeremy shook his head. "What about the sirens? Have they been causing problems again?" He looked at me. "They sometimes sing too loudly late at night."

"They've disappeared," Conway explained. "Every single one of them. Nerita's been looking for them everywhere or so she claims. Father doesn't know they've gone and Nerita is doing her best to keep that information from him." He frowned. "I thought that's why you were here, Cassia. I thought you'd heard about them. I think their disappearance has something to do with that black cloud that hung over our sea about a month ago."

For the second time that day, my blood ran cold. I said, "Tell me more about that cloud."

"It came from Brimstone town one morning. It hovered over the sea for two days and then rain came from it. It wasn't like normal rain; it was black. It rained over one area of the sea for about an hour until the cloud melted away."

In my arms, Stanley said, "Cassia, that cloud must have been filled with black magic."

27

Conway's perfect brow wrinkled. "Black magic?"

I nodded. "It infected Brimstone town. Blythe got rid of it recently. Some of it must have made its way over to you." I looked over my shoulder towards the sea. "Whereabouts did the rain go? Has anyone checked that area beneath the sea?" I looked back at Conway.

He nodded. "Nerita checked it immediately." He paused and looked towards the sea again. "The area beneath the black cloud was where the sirens lived. Do you think they were affected by the black magic?"

"I don't know. It does seem a coincidence that they've now disappeared. Do you have any idea where they might have gone?"

Conway moved closer to me and lowered his voice. "I've been thinking about that. What if they've somehow found a way into your world, Cassia?"

"My world? How? Why would they want to do that?"

Jeremy took a sharp intake of breath and said, "If they have been infected with the black magic and made their way into your world, they'll cause havoc. Sirens haven't been allowed into your world for hundreds of years, and for good reason too."

Stanley snuggled closer to me. "Cassia, I don't like the sound of this. What do sirens do? I don't know anything about them."

Conway said, "They find sailors and target them. They sing mournful songs which lure the sailors into the sea."

Stanley gulped. "And then what?"

"They kill them," Conway finished.

In a hesitant tone, I asked, "How many sirens have left your sea?"

"Over a hundred." Conway gave me a fearful look. "Cassia, can you do something about this? Before it's too late?"

Chapter 6

I couldn't look away from the expanse of sea. The thought of over a hundred sirens making their way into my world with murderous thoughts in their heads wasn't fully registering in my brain. I felt a hand on my elbow and looked that way.

Conway gave me a gentle smile. "Perhaps we should have a sit-down and discuss this? I might be able to help you in some way. Shall we go to the café?"

I nodded numbly. With Gran and Blythe gone, it would be up to me to stop those sirens. But how? Where would I start looking?

I allowed Conway to steer me towards the café. My arms were shaking slightly and Jeremy took Stanley from me. With each step on the sand, the responsibility on my shoulders felt heavier and heavier.

When we entered the open-air café, my spirits lifted somewhat at the welcome sight of a familiar face. I hesitated. She did look familiar, but I was almost sure I'd never met her before. I scanned the tall, slim creature who was gliding towards us with a welcoming look on her face. Her long dress brushed the sandy floor as she moved.

From Jeremy's arms, Stanley said, "Cassia, she looks like Gilda from the Mooncrest Café. But a bit older."

The creature let out a gentle laugh. "I am a few years older than Gilda." She pointed to the tiny lines around her eyes. "These give me away. Gilda is my younger sister. I believe you've met our other sister, Gisela. She runs The Razzle Dazzle club in Brimstone. I'm Gia, the old one of the bunch." She placed a warm hand on my shoulder. "I know who you are, Cassia. Gilda has kept me up to date with your investigations in Brimstone. I knew your mum well. She often came here to think. You came with her sometimes when you were little. I know exactly what to get you. Please, take a seat and I'll return shortly." She smiled before gliding away.

Stanley and I were regular visitors to the Mooncrest Café and Gilda was a good friend. She had a special talent for knowing precisely what you needed to eat and drink. I'd met her sister, Gisela, when I'd investigation the murder of a vampire a while back. Gisela had the same talent as Gilda for knowing what I needed to drink and had brought me an amazing drink which I still dreamt about. It looked like their older sister had the same gift too.

Stanley said, "Cassia, look at the sand. Gia isn't leaving any footprints as she moves along. How do they do it?" He looked up at Jeremy. "Do you know how they do it? How do Gilda and her sisters move? Do they glide across the floor on air? Are they magic? What sort of creatures are they? Cassia has been meaning to ask Gilda, but she's been too polite to do so."

"Stanley," I said with more than a touch of embarrassment in my voice. "It's none of our business what kind of creatures they are." I shot a cursory glance at Jeremy. "Unless you do know? Do you?"

Jeremy opened his mouth and then shut it. He shrugged. "I've no idea. I've been meaning to ask Gia too, but it seemed rude to do so."

We all turned our nosy faces to Conway.

He frowned, looked at Gia as she busied herself behind the counter and then shook his head.

We made our way over to a table which looked out across the beach. Gia returned with bowls of ice cream for us. The ice cream was white with tiny silver and gold stars sprinkled on the top. Butterfly-shaped chocolate pieces stuck out of the ice cream.

Gia said, "Everything is edible including the stars. Stanley, this is for you." She whipped out a small blanket from somewhere behind her and placed it on the sandy floor. She put a bowl down on it and smiled over at Stanley. "Fish-flavoured ice cream. I hope you like it."

Stanley's little pink tongue shot out and he licked his lips. He was out of Jeremy's arms and on the blanket in a nanosecond.

I wanted to question Conway about the missing sirens, but my attention was fully drawn to the ice cream. A gentle memory stirred in my mind. I saw an image of being here with Mum. We used to share a bowl of this very same ice cream. I picked up my spoon and scooped up a small amount. As soon as I put it in my mouth, the image in my mind intensified. I saw Mum smiling down at me and tucking a piece of my hair behind my ear. I heard her asking if I wanted any more or if I'd had enough. I heard my own reply of 'More, please!' followed by Mum's lovely laugh. I continued eating as the memory filled my heart to overflowing.

When I'd finished the last of the ice cream, I put my spoon down and leant back in my seat. Jeremy and Conway were staring at me with their mouths open. Neither had touched their bowls of ice cream.

"What's wrong with you two?" I asked. "Eat up. It's delicious."

Jeremy's voice was hoarse as he said, "You glowed. When you were eating just now, you glowed. It was like a pink cloud had surrounded you. It was beautiful. How did you make that happen?"

I felt my cheeks warming up. "I was thinking about Mum. I remembered our time here together. It made me feel all warm and fuzzy inside."

Conway pushed his bowl of ice cream towards me. "How wonderful. Here; have mine."

I was tempted, but I didn't want to look like a greedy-guts in front of him. I pushed the bowl back and said, "No, thank you. Tell me more about what's been going on with the sirens. Has there been any other unusual activity? Jeremy said he picked up on an uneasy atmosphere."

Jeremy nodded as he picked up his spoon. "It's like something terrible is going to happen." He put some of the ice cream in his mouth. His eyes closed and he let out a sigh of appreciation. He opened his eyes and said, "I might need to order another bowl of this."

Conway said, "There has been a strange feeling amongst everyone here recently. I put it down to that black cloud and Nerita shouting at everyone more than usual. I can talk to Nerita on your behalf and see what she knows about the sirens, if that's okay? I have tried to talk to her before about it, but she tells me it's none of my business. I can tell she's worried about something, though."

"If you don't mind me asking, who is in charge of your people? Is it your father?" I asked.

Conway nodded. "Yes, but Nerita does most of the work now. I do what I can but Nerita likes to take control of everything."

I was about to ask him another question when I felt someone standing behind me. I looked over my shoulder and saw a mermaid there. She had long, golden hair which was pinned up on one side by a beautiful comb which sparkled and twinkled with many small, silver stones which were embedded in it.

She smiled at me and said, "Sorry to disturb you. I hope you don't mind if I say something about Nerita?" Without waiting for an answer, she pulled a chair over and sat at my side.

Conway said, "Isla, this isn't the time. I've already told Cassia about the black cloud and the missing sirens."

Isla gave him a sweet smile. "Have you told her everything? Have you told her about the secret meetings your sister had with the sirens before they went missing?"

Conway's fingers clenched around the spoon he was holding. "Isla, you know that's only a rumour. I asked Nerita about that, and she denied it."

"She would, wouldn't she?" Isla gave me her full attention. "I'm Conway's betrothed. I've known Nerita long enough to see how badly she treats Conway. Just because she's older than him, she thinks she can get away with treating him as if he's worth nothing. She never gives him any responsibility in the sea. He's more than capable of helping her rule over everyone when King Taron passes on. She's been having secret meetings with the sirens for weeks. It wouldn't surprise me if she ordered the sirens to _"

Conway dropped his spoon and got to his feet. "Isla! That's enough. Those are rumours. I told you not to listen to gossip about my sister." He held his hand out to her. "Come on, let's go for a swim. I've been out of the water too long."

Isla hesitated before standing up and taking his hand.

Conway looked at me and said, "Will you investigate the disappearance of the sirens, please? Don't tell my father; I don't want him to worry. I'll speak more forcibly to Nerita and see what she knows about them. Thank you."

He walked out of the café holding Isla's hand tightly.

I watched them go. "Well, Jeremy, what do you think about that?"

Jeremy replied, "I think I'm going to have Conway's ice cream. There's no point letting it go to waste." He pulled Conway's bowl towards him and stuck his spoon into the melting mixture.

I shook my head at him. "What's going on with Isla? What are the rumours about Nerita?"

"Isla doesn't like Nerita. She wants Conway to be in charge. Then when they get married, she would become queen." He shoved a large amount of ice cream into his mouth. Some of it dribbled down his chin. I picked up a serviette and passed it to him.

Stanley suddenly leapt onto my knee. His eyes were wide with fright. "Cassia! The sea! Look at it! It's coming to get us."

I looked out and saw a huge wall of water rising up from the sea. It rose higher and higher. The watery wall blotted out the sun. There was a roar which sounded like animals roaring.

The wall stopped going upwards. It was still for one second, then it raced towards us.

Stanley screamed. So did I. I urgently sent magic to my fingers and scanned my brain for the appropriate spell. I couldn't find one. I glanced at Jeremy who was watching the rushing water with a small amount of interest.

"Do something!" I yelled at him.

He waved his spoon in the air. "There's nothing anyone can do. Watch what happens. You're going to love this."

Chapter 7

Stanley quivered on my knee as we stared at the massive wall of water. The noise it made changed from a roar to a cacophony of neighs.

Neighs? I shared a look with Stanley. He tipped his head as if trying to make sense of the new noise.

The white foam at the edge of the water began to change into something else. I saw a hoof, and then a leg, followed by many more hooves and legs. Horse legs?

Stanley and I watched in astonishment as the water transformed into white horses running up the beach. As if that wasn't startling enough, the horses then changed into tall, muscular men with flowing white hair. They were naked apart from a pair of long, white shorts stretched across their thick, muscular legs. They stopped running and came to a slow walk. Some turned to chat to each other and some looked along the beach as if searching for something. A tall man at the front stared right at us and headed our way.

I said to Jeremy, "What was that? How did that happen? Who are they?"

"What are they?" Stanley added. "They came right out of the water like magic. Where did the horses go?"

Jeremy pushed his second bowl of ice cream to one side. It was now empty. He said, "They are kelpies. Haven't you ever heard of them? They're shapeshifting water creatures. They patrol the seas as water horses and then turn into human form on land." He looked down at his empty bowls. "I think I might be able to squeeze in another bowl. What do you think?"

I stared out at the kelpies. The sun shone brightly on them and picked out every firm jawline and taut muscle. I thought the merpeople were magnificent to look at, but the kelpies took perfection to another level.

Stanley nudged his head into my arm and whispered, "Cassia, your mouth is hanging open and you're drooling a bit. It's not a good look."

I snapped my mouth shut just in time as the tall kelpie reached the café and strode over to our table.

His long hair settled in perfect waves around his face like a horse's mane. Well, I suppose it would do, wouldn't it? His features looked as if they'd been chiselled onto his face by a skilled artist.

He stopped at our table, gave me a tight smile and stuck his hand out. "Cassia Winter? I'm Rex, the leader of the Brimstone kelpies. I'm here to carry out your orders. What would you like me to do?"

I put my hand in his and tried not to wince at his strong handshake. He was here to carry out my orders? I don't know why, but I thought about the garden back at Gran's house. I'd been meaning to clear out the old shed for months now. And there was the decorating in the bathroom. That had been on my list for a while. As for the windows! That window cleaner Gran employed never reached the corners. I could do with someone going up a ladder and giving them a good going over.

Rex released my hand and said, "I know what you're thinking. You'd like me and my colleagues to investigate the disappearance of the sirens."

I gave him a slow nod. "Right. Yes. That's exactly what I was thinking. Won't you sit down?"

Rex pulled out the chair next to Jeremy and lowered his impressive body into it. The chair creaked under the weight of his many muscles. Rex looked Jeremy's way and nodded in acknowledgement. "Jeremy."

Jeremy smiled at him. "Nice to see you again, Rex. Do you fancy some ice cream? I know I shouldn't have any more, but I can't resist." He looked over his shoulder at Gia and gave her a wave.

Rex put a hand on his taut stomach. "You know I don't eat refined food, and you shouldn't either. It dulls the brain. It stops you from making wise choices."

Jeremy shrugged and then mouthed an order for more ice cream to Gia.

I was tempted to ask for more too, but I didn't want Rex to think my brain was going to be too dull to give him orders about the sirens. I wasn't sure what those orders were going to be yet, but I wanted to stay sharp.

Rex turned his light, green eyes on me. His tone softened, "I knew your mum. I helped her with her work here. She was an amazing woman. You look like her."

"Thank you. I'm hearing a lot about my mum today. You'll have to forgive me, but up until a short while ago, I didn't know this beach existed. I spoke to Conway a few minutes ago and he told me about the missing sirens. What do you know about them?"

"I know they're missing and that they're nowhere to be found around here. I've been searching for them for days now." He hesitated a fraction. "Discreetly, of course."

"Why discreetly?"

"Because of Nerita. She knows the sirens are missing and she's looking for them on her own. She ordered me to stop searching for them. She feels responsible that they've gone missing."

I asked, "Why does she think that? I've heard she'd been meeting with them recently. Is that true?"

"I'm not sure about that," Rex replied. "Nerita keeps herself to herself a lot of the time. Her father, King Taron, is getting weaker by the day and it'll be time for him to give up his throne soon. That's going to be a lot of responsibility for Nerita and she's already taking on some of the king's duties. She's a stubborn individual and won't let anyone help her. Not me, and not her brother."

Gia quietly arrived with another bowl of ice cream for Jeremy. She placed a cup of tea in front of me. I gave her a grateful smile. A cup of tea was just what I needed. Gia winked before silently moving away.

I said to Rex, "Why do you need me to give you orders about the sirens?"

"You can overrule Nerita. As a justice witch, you have the power to do that."

"Do I?"

Rex nodded. "Your mum had the same authority. She had to assert her powers now and again with certain creatures around here." His look turned more serious. "Cassia, we need to know where the sirens have gone, and why they left Brimstone Beach. Nerita is doing her best to look for them, but we can help her if we have your authority. She doesn't have to know, we can continue to be discreet. If we have your authority, we can question the sea creatures too. The sirens have never gone missing before and I'm concerned."

With bits of ice cream around his mouth, Jeremy said, "I'm concerned too. The sirens need to be found as soon as possible."

"Well?" Rex waited for my answer.

I took a sip of tea and immediately felt Mum's presence again. I suddenly recalled how she'd let me have my own cup of tea whenever she had one. She made sure it was lukewarm before giving it to me. I instinctively knew what Mum would say.

"Rex, I'd like you to investigate the disappearance of the sirens. If you run into Nerita, let her know that I've told you to do so. Report straight back to me. Thank you."

The admiration in Rex's eyes made me feel warm and I knew I'd said the right thing.

Rex said, "You've made the right decision. I'll be in touch soon." He gave me a nod, stood up and strode purposefully away.

Stanley said, "I like him. He smells strong and brave."

We watched Rex as he walked over to his colleagues and began to talk to them. When he'd finished talking, they turned back into white horses and galloped into the sea. I was half expecting them to transform into huge waves again, but they didn't. They kept galloping into the water until their heads disappeared beneath the sea.

I said to Jeremy, "What do you think is going on with the sirens? Has anything like this ever happened before?"

He shook his head and put his empty bowl next to the other two empty ones. "I can't help feeling that something terrible is going to happen soon. Can you feel it too?"

Despite the heat of the day and the warmth of the tea in my stomach, I shivered. I said, "I can feel that. I can feel something else too. It's like events have already been put in motion and there's nothing I can do to stop them."

Chapter 8

As if sensing my unease, dark clouds moved across the sky and blotted out the sun.

Jeremy looked skywards and said, "It's going to rain. There's nothing more miserable than rain when you're at the beach."

I glanced at the merpeople who were now packing up their belongings. "Are they leaving?"

Jeremy nodded. "They'll return to the sea for a while. Do you want to talk to them?"

"I do. I wanted to get to know them a bit better before asking about the sirens."

I watched a group of merpeople walk to the edge of the water and wade in. As soon as they were chest high in the water, they dipped under it and I saw tails flipping up and catching the last rays of the sun as it vanished behind the grey clouds.

Gia came over to us and said, "I'm going to start putting the café walls up to stop the rain coming in. I'll keep the café open in case anyone wants a hot drink. Do you want anything else?"

I shook my head. "We'll head back to Brimstone for now, but we'll come back later."

Gia said, "Say hello to Gilda for me. She hasn't been over here for a visit for a long time and I know she misses the beach." She glanced towards the sandy beach. "Could you take her a shell back, please? One of the round, silver ones. They're magical and they carry the sounds of this beach with them. Gilda would love that. I'll go and find one for you."

Stanley leapt off my lap and declared, "I've seen some of those shells. I'll find a good one for you." He scampered off with an eager look on his furry face.

I called out, "Stay away from the water's edge!"

"Will do!" Stanley shouted back.

Stanley came back a minute later with a beautiful silver shell in his mouth. He dropped it at Gia's feet and smiled up at her.

Gia picked it up and nodded in approval. "Perfect. Just perfect. Thank you, Stanley. Would you like some fish ice cream to go? I can put it in a special container so that it doesn't melt."

"I would love that! Thank you."

Jeremy noisily cleared his throat.

I said, "Could we have some too, please?"

Jeremy cleared his throat again.

I added, "Not the fish one, the one you gave us before."

Gia smiled. "I'll sort that out immediately."

As soon as we had our ice cream tubs, we said thank you and goodbye to Gia and then took to the grey skies on our broomsticks. I insisted Stanley sit with me as I still hadn't fully got over the shock of him almost drowning.

The beach was completely deserted by the time we left. The rain had started and soft drops landed on the sand like tears. I looked away from the depressing sight and rose above the clouds until we came to blue sky. One of the perks of having a broomstick.

We were silent as we flew back to Brimstone. My stomach was in knots about leaving the beach. I knew something terrible was going to happen, but I also knew I couldn't stop it. It was an awful feeling and I couldn't shake it at all.

The clouds beneath us drifted away as we reached the town leaving us with a clear sky.

We went straight to the apartment that Gran has in town as I wanted to put the ice cream in the freezer before Jeremy gobbled it all up. I'd seen how he'd been looking at the tubs on our return flight.

Gran's apartment was located over the Mooncrest Café. It had a spacious living area with a small kitchen to one side. The best thing about the apartment was the huge windows which overlooked the town square. The windows were tinted and Stanley and I had spent a lot of time staring out at the residents of Brimstone in the safe knowledge that they couldn't see us spying on them.

As soon as Jeremy came into the apartment, he clasped his hands together and said, "This is magnificent. Wow. What a lovely place for you to hang out in." He scanned left and right. "A fully stocked bookcase. Perfect. DVDs. Super. Is that the full series of Murder, She Wrote? I watched them with your mum sometimes. Between you and me, I have a crush on Angela Lansbury."

"Where did you watch them with Mum?" I asked. "Here?"

Jeremy didn't answer as he moved swiftly over to the windows and pressed his face against one of them. "Who is that over there? Is he a vampire?" He squinted. "I can't see his fangs properly. Who's he talking to? Is that a goblin or a gnome?"

Stanley trotted over to his side and said helpfully, "There are some binoculars over there at your side. Cassia uses them all the time. I've got some too." He moved over to where his cat-sized binoculars had been fixed to the window sill at the perfect height for him. He peered through and said, "Jeremy, look to your left. That's a garden gnome. She's called Mrs Tarblast. I can tell you a thing or two about her if you don't mind a bit of gossip?"

"I never mind a bit of gossip." Jeremy located the binoculars, shuffled over to Stanley and peered out at the residents of Brimstone. Stanley proceeded to tell him everything he knew about the creatures outside.

I propped the broomsticks against the wall near the door. Jeremy had dropped his in excitement the second he'd entered the apartment. I took the ice cream tubs over to the freezer and put them in. I checked the contents of the fridge to see if I needed to buy anything. I had a feeling we wouldn't be returning to Gran's house until this business with the sirens was settled.

I smiled when I saw the fridge was stocked with everything we needed. Gilda had access to this apartment and she always knew when Stanley and I would be returning for a while.

That reminded me.

I walked over to the spies at the window and said, "When you've quite finished gossiping about everyone, I'd like to call on Gilda and give her that shell."

Jeremy immediately lowered his binoculars. "Gilda! The Mooncrest Café! I haven't been there for years." He patted his stomach. "I think I could manage a snack or two."

I took in his skinny frame. "Where do you put it all?"

He shrugged. "I don't know. I can eat what I want and stay thin."

I shook my head at him. "That's so annoying. It's a good job I like you. Come on."

We left the apartment and headed downstairs to the café. Stanley insisted on carrying the shell in his mouth. As we entered the café, he padded over to Gilda and proudly dropped the shell in front of her.

Gilda picked it up with a quizzical expression on her face.

I followed Stanley and explained to Gilda about our visit to the beach.

Jeremy stepped forward and gave Gilda a big hug. He said, "It's so good to see you again. You smell delicious."

Gilda laughed as she was released from his hug. "You are one of my favourite customers, Jeremy Spring. You never leave anything on your plate. Could you manage something to eat now? I know you've had some of my sister's ice cream. I can smell it on you."

Jeremy said, "Perhaps a snack or two, just to be polite. Thank you."

Gilda nodded and then put the shell to her ear. She sighed happily. "I'd forgotten how soothing it is to hear the sea. I can't hear anyone talking, but I can hear the sound of the rain. Is it raining now?"

I frowned. "It was when we left. How can you hear the rain through that shell?"

"It's a Brimstone shell. It's magical," Gilda explained. "It picks up on sounds that are going on right now." She smiled. "I can hear Gia singing in the distance. Take a seat and I'll bring you something over." She glided away with the shell pressed against her ear and a smile on her face.

I took Jeremy over to my favourite table. It was next to the window which gave me a view of the town and also a view of the rest of the café.

As we sat down, the café door opened and Luca entered. He immediately looked our way and I saw his nostrils flaring as if he'd just smelled something revolting.

Stanley called out from my lap, "Luca! We're over here. We've been to the beach. I nearly drowned!"

I hissed, "Stanley, he's not our friend at the moment. He doesn't know who we are."

Stanley's head dropped. "I forgot."

Luca stared at Stanley and I saw a flicker of concern in his eyes. Just as abruptly, it was gone. He hesitated as if he wasn't sure how he should respond to Stanley's outburst.

Jeremy got swiftly to his feet and walked over to Luca. He grabbed his hand and shook it. "I'm Jeremy Spring. I don't think we've ever met. I believe you're a guardian in this town. Is that right?"

Luca gave him a reluctant nod and cast a hostile look my way.

Jeremy continued brightly, "In that case, I'm sure you'd like to hear about Cassia's latest case. Well, it's not really a case yet but we suspect it will turn into one. Join us at the table and we'll fill you in."

"No, thank you," Luca replied curtly.

Jeremy wasn't put off by Luca's cold attitude and told him briefly what we'd been up to.

Luca listened silently with no expression on his face. When Jeremy came to the bit about the grindylows grabbing Stanley, the concern came into Luca's eyes again and he gave Stanley a curious look.

When Jeremy had finished, Luca said coldly, "Thanks for telling me. The Brimstone beach is not my concern." He gave Stanley another quizzical look before abruptly walking out of the café.

Jeremy shook his head at his departure and returned to our table. He said, "Thanks to the spell Astrid put on him, Luca does not like you one little bit. There is intense hate for you, Cassia. I could almost taste it."

I nodded. "I know."

"His hate is a temporary thing, I felt that too. It's not stable and keeps wavering. Did you see how he looked at Stanley? It was like he knew him, but he didn't know how he knew him."

"I noticed that," Stanley said. His tone was hopeful as he continued, "I think he remembers me. Somewhere in the back of his mind, I think he remembers his good friend, Stanley."

I stroked Stanley's head. "I hope you're right, but don't be disappointed if you're not."

"I'll try not to."

Jeremy looked over my shoulder and rubbed his hands together. "Gilda's coming back." His expression changed and his hands dropped to his lap. "Something's wrong."

Gilda's face was even paler than usual as she came to our table. Her hand trembled as she gave me the shell. "Cassia, listen."

I put the shell to my ear and heard Gia cry out, "She's dead! Nerita's dead!"

Chapter 9

Jeremy, Stanley and I rushed back to Brimstone Beach as quickly as our broomsticks would allow. From the air, we saw a group of merpeople clustered around a cave a short distance from the café. We landed behind the merpeople who moved out of the way when they recognised us.

I placed my broomstick at the entrance to the cave and walked slowly in. There was a stillness inside as if the cave were holding its breath. I felt like doing the same. I could feel Stanley's fur brushing my legs as he walked slowly at my side. Jeremy was right behind us.

There was a tailed figure lying on the sand near the back of the cave. As I walked closer, the top part of the body came into view. I recognised the short, spiky hair on the motionless head. Nerita's eyes were open and she stared unseeing at the cave roof. Her face was white and her left hand was resting on her throat.

I didn't want to move too close and contaminate the scene. I whispered to Jeremy, "What's happened to her? Why is she in her mermaid form so far from the sea?"

Jeremy replied, "I don't know. Merpeople don't change into their tails until they're in the sea. It's dangerous for them to be in this form on land as they can't breathe properly." He crouched at Nerita's side and looked closer at her face. "It looks like she was struggling to breathe. You can see how her left hand has clawed at her throat, possibly in terror. I don't understand why she changed into her tailed self so far from the sea."

I crouched next to Jeremy and kept my voice low, "Would something or someone have caused her to change into her present form? Could someone have forced her to do it?"

Jeremy looked into my eyes and gave me a slight nod. It seems he was just aware as me of the merpeople behind us who were listening to our words. He whispered, "This must be the dreadful thing I've been expecting." He shook his head sorrowfully. "I didn't think it was going to be this, though. Poor Nerita."

Stanley was sniffing the sand. He looked at me and said, "Something doesn't smell right." He moved carefully along, still sniffing. He stopped at the side of a small rock and popped his head behind it. "Cassia, there's something here. Come and have a look."

I went over to Stanley and saw what he was looking at. I used a tissue from my pocket to pick up the bottle of water which had been half buried in the sand. Brimstone didn't have facilities for checking fingerprints yet, but I was hoping I could sort something out in the future. I'd bought something off Amazon which would allow me to highlight fingerprints on objects. It wasn't much of a start to my forensics department, but it was something.

I took the bottle over to Jeremy and showed him it.

He straightened up and said, "That's saltwater. All the merpeople drink that. Gia sells it at the café."

"Why do they drink saltwater?" I asked. "And why would they buy it from Gia if there's an ocean full of it out there?"

"Gia filters it first to get rid of any contamination and then she chills it. I don't know why it's been left in this cave. Merpeople always take their empty bottles back to Gia."

I held the bottle up. It was half full. I said, "What would happen if they drank normal water? Like the water you and I would drink?"

Jeremy's eyes widened. "It would be like poison to them."

"What exactly would it do to them? Would it…?" I sent a pointed look towards Nerita's lifeless body.

Jeremy gave me a slow nod. "It would. The water would cause an immediate change in them from legs to a tail. But we don't know if it is pure water in that bottle. The label says that it's seawater. Gia is very careful to keep her bottles of water clearly labelled and in different places in the café."

Using the tissue, I took the lid off the bottle and sniffed the liquid inside. I don't know what I was expecting, but I didn't get an aroma of anything. I lifted the bottle.

Stanley yelled, "Cassia! Don't drink it! It could have poison in it."

There was a collective gasp behind me from the merpeople.

Someone called out, "Nerita has been poisoned! She's been murdered!"

I looked over at the crowd and said calmly, "We don't know that yet." I turned back to Jeremy. "We need to get this water analysed. Dr Morgan can do that for us. I'd like her to look at the body too. I don't suppose there are any butterflies around here ready to take a message to the doctor?"

Jeremy said, "I can summon one. That's the wonderful thing about your Brimstone butterflies; they are always on call, no matter how far away you are. I'll go outside and summon one now." He turned away from me and swiftly left the cave.

I was putting the lid back on the bottle when a someone came running through the cave yelling, "My sister! Where's my sister?"

Conway came to an abrupt halt when he saw Nerita lying on the sand. His face turned as pale as hers. "No!" he wailed. "No! This can't be! She can't be dead." He turned his stricken face to me and his glance went to the bottle in my hand. "What is that? Has it got something to do with Nerita? What's in it?"

"I don't know yet." I wrapped the tissue fully around the bottle and lay a hand on Conway's elbow. "I'm sorry about your sister. I will find out what happened to her. You must leave this area now. I want to examine it fully."

Conway looked back at Nerita and tears escaped from his eyes. "I can't leave her lying here on her own." He blinked rapidly. "Father. What will I tell Father? His heart will break when he hears about Nerita. What will we do without her?" His voice caught in his throat and more tears flowed down his face.

I gently steered him out of the cave. The crowd of merpeople moved to one side and their heads hung low. As I walked through them, I was dismayed to see many footprints in the sand. That wouldn't help my investigation at all.

Isla came rushing towards him. She pulled him into her embrace and patted his back. "Conway, I've just heard the terrible news. You poor thing. You must stay strong at this awful time. You have to be in control. Your people need you to be strong. You must take over Nerita's duties and obligations immediately."

Conway untangled himself. "Isla, I can't think about things like that now."

She stared intensely into his eyes. "You have to. You have to think about the future. Your sister has gone. Your father is too old to do anything any longer. You have to accept your responsibilities. Don't worry, I will help you. I'll be right at your side." She placed her hand on the sparkling comb in her hair and patted it. "It's time for us to think about our future. I'll deal with things now. You must go and talk to your father immediately." She led him away from me and pushed him in the direction of the sea.

Conway looked too shocked to argue with her. His head was low as he dragged his feet towards the sea. Isla watched him go and then walked towards the cave.

I jogged after him and said, "I can speak to your father if you like? Ask him to come here and I'll reassure him that I'm looking into how Nerita died."

Conway's voice held no emotion as he said, "I can't do that. Father never leaves the sea. I'll be alright. I have to be." He didn't look my way as he walked slowly into the water.

I heard raised voices behind me and quickly returned to the cave. Isla had her hands on her hips and was glowering at the sobbing merpeople in front of her.

Isla ordered, "Don't stand there crying. There's work to be done. I'm in charge now until Conway's sorted himself out."

I moved in front of Isla and said, "This is a time for grieving. I don't know how your ruling system works, but I do know that I have authority over your people." My voice wavered. Was that right? Or did I just have authority when it came to justice work?

Isla looked unsure at my words. I steadied my gaze and tried to look as serious as I could.

Isla folded her arms. "How long are they going to take to grieve? There's business to attend to."

"That can wait. I'm investigating Nerita's death and that could take a while. I'll be interviewing everyone." I noticed Isla's gaze slipping to the left. I added, "Including you. Where were you at the time of Nerita's death?"

Isla looked back at me. "I don't know. What time did she die?"

I paused and then admitted the truth. "I don't know yet. I'll ask you again when I do know. Did Nerita have any enemies?"

"Yeah, plenty. Me included. She was a bossy mermaid who ordered everyone around. She tried to take over King Taron's job before he was ready to retire. Conway would have done a better job of ruling our people. I told Nerita that many times. I told her to share her duties with him, but she never listened to me." She patted the comb in her hair again. "Conway will be taking over now. As his future wife, I'll be helping him. Have you got any more questions for me? I want to see if Conway's told his father yet. I've got plans for my people and this beach."

"Your people?" I felt my eyebrows rising in surprise.

Isla let out a nervous laugh. "Oops. I'm getting ahead of myself. Can I go? Everyone else has gone back to the sea."

I looked over my shoulder to see she was right. The merpeople had all returned to the sea. Heck. I hadn't taken the opportunity to make a list of their names. I really must hone up on my investigation skills.

Isla was already halfway down the sand when I looked back. I sighed. I'd catch up with her later.

Gia came floating over the sand with a roll of ribbon in her hand. She said sadly, "I thought you might need this to cordon the cave off. Your mum used it sometimes when she was investigating an injustice. Would you like me to help you put it up? I've also brought a sign that your mum used."

I looked at the sign that Gia took from her pocket. I had letters and cards at home which Mum had written to me so I recognised her handwriting. The sign told creatures of all species to keep away from the cordoned-off area. There was a polite thank you on the end of the sign which made me smile.

Once the cave had been secured, I asked Gia about Nerita and whether she had any enemies.

Gia said, "I wouldn't say enemies as such. She was a strong-willed mermaid who was determined to do her job well. She took her responsibilities seriously and a lot of merpeople didn't like that. Especially Isla. Nerita often gave her security work to do at the outer boundaries of the sea. There are a few krakens and sea serpents out there who don't obey the rules and like to cause havoc. The merpeople have to keep them in check. Isla didn't like that kind of work and preferred sunning herself on the beach with her friends."

I told Gia about the water bottle and added, "I'm going to get the water analysed. How easy would it be for someone to put pure water in a saltwater bottle?"

"I suppose it would be easy enough for someone to do that as I have a tap of clear water on that wall behind my café." She pointed towards a small wall which had a silver tap halfway up it. "There's a warning sign above it and all the merpeople know to keep away from it. Even a drop of pure water could hurt them. If someone did put pure water in that bottle, I don't think it would be a merperson because they would put themselves at considerable risk by going near that tap."

Jeremy came jogging across the sand to us. He said, "I've sent a message to the doctor. I've already received a reply to say she's on her way."

"Thank you." I looked towards the sea. "I'd really like to speak to Nerita's father. Do you think he could be persuaded to come onto the beach?"

Gia shook her head. "No. But you can go to his palace, can't you? Your mum used to do that when needed. She used magic on herself so she could breathe underwater."

Jeremy clicked his fingers. "The underwater spell! Of course. I know how to do that. Cassia, do you want to give it a go? You might feel as if you're about to drown, but that feeling should pass eventually." He gave me a big smile of encouragement. "And if you do actually start to drown, I'll pull you to safety."

I looked down at Stanley. He said, "I'm not going back into the water. Those grindylows will be after me again." He lifted his chin and I saw the slight tremble there. "Unless you want me to go with you? I can do that. If you really want me to."

I picked him up and cuddled him. "I won't ask you to do that. You stay here while I go in the water with Jeremy."

Gia held her arms out. "I can look after Stanley. I made far too much fish ice cream earlier. It needs using up."

Stanley said, "Thank you, but I think I need to be brave and help Cassia."

I passed Stanley over to Gia and said, "Stanley, you don't have to do that. You stay here and keep dry. I'll be back soon."

Stanley looked at me for a moment and then said, "Okay. Don't be long. Take care. Please don't drown."

"I won't." I stroked Stanley's head and gave him a reassuring smile.

Jeremy led me to the water's edge. He rolled his sleeves up and said, "I hope I've got the right words. Your mum used to say the words and I wasn't always paying attention when she performed this spell." He pressed his lips together, thought for a while and then nodded. "Yes, I'm sure we'll be fine."

Chapter 10

Jeremy mumbled something and then waved his arms over himself and me. He tutted, shook his head and muttered something about that being a spell for everlasting sleep. He started with his mumblings again and flapped his arms in my direction. My confidence in his spell casting capabilities decreased by the second.

Jeremy eventually gave me a satisfied nod. "That should do. By the way, are you a strong swimmer?"

"Not really. Just average, I suppose."

"Ah. But you can float? You must be able to float. Everyone can float. Can't they?" He grinned at me. "Let's give this a go." He made a move towards the water.

I pulled at my T-shirt. "What do we do about our clothes? Will they stay dry or should I take some items off?"

"They won't stay dry, but you can strip down to your underwear if you like?"

With one thing and another, I hadn't had the opportunity to do a full wash of my clothes and I was now down to the underwear which had seen many better days. I was wearing my slightly grey, slightly baggy underwear now, and no one needed to see that.

I shook my head at Jeremy. "I don't mind them getting wet. I can use my magic drying hands on myself afterwards." I almost felt like adding 'if we survive' but I didn't want to upset Jeremy.

I took my shoes and socks off before following Jeremy as I didn't want them weighing me down. As I did so, I said, "What's going to happen to us? How are we going to breathe underwater?"

Jeremy moved his hand over my head and face. "There's an invisible barrier here. It continually fills with fresh air. It's like one of those old-fashioned diving helmets that people used to wear, but it's lighter and much more efficient. Just breathe normally when we go under the water. The worst thing you can do is panic."

"Okay." My heart was already thudding in my chest and panic was settling in my stomach and getting ready to grow. I took some deep breaths before moving further into the warm water. I reminded myself why I was doing this. There had been a murder and it was my responsibility to find the creature who had committed it.

Jeremy walked briskly forwards and dipped under the water. I followed him and as I fully submerged myself, I started to swim. My instinct was to hold my breath, but I forced myself to breathe normally. It wasn't an easy thing to do and my mind was telling me to get back out of the water.

Jeremy looked over his shoulder at me and said, "How are you doing? Are you breathing normally? Speak to me. That will show me that your breathing is normal."

I opened my mouth to talk and fully expected water to come rushing in. It didn't, but I did get a waft of cold air coming in. I said, "I think I'm okay. How long does this spell last?"

"A good hour or so." He smiled. "I wasn't sure I had the right words for this spell. I surprised myself! Follow me. I know where King Taron lives."

I swam downwards. Now that I'd got used to breathing underwater, I started to look around me at the beautiful sea creatures swimming along. I saw multi-coloured seahorses bobbing next to me. Fish of all colours darted around me as if they were in a rush to get somewhere. Crabs scrabbled over rocks beneath me and a starfish was trying to hide behind a piece of pink coral. Seaweed drifted on the current and gently curled around my hand.

Jeremy shouted, "Cassia! The grindylows have got you!"

The seaweed on my hand tightened and I was pulled to one side. I saw that the seaweed was actually a small green creature. It had an impish face with wide, blue eyes and a cheeky smile. Its limbs were long and floaty giving the impression of loose seaweed. Another grindylow was behind that one and it reached out a green hand to me.

"Come and play with us," the first grindylow said in a childlike voice. "We want to play. We want to talk to you."

I tried to pull my hand free. "No, thank you. I don't have time to play."

The smile fell from the grindylow's face. "But I want to tell you something. Come and play with us."

Jeremy darted to my side and raised his hands at the little creatures. "Be gone!" he boomed. "Now!"

The grindylows yelped and swiftly turned away from us. They swam away and I could have sworn I heard them crying. They sounded like children.

"Jeremy, you didn't have to shout at them. You scared them."

"You don't know what they're like. They'll trick you into playing games down here until your air runs out."

"But they said they had something to tell me. It could have been something important."

Jeremy shook his head. "It's a trick to get you to go with them. Come on; we're not far from King Taron's palace now."

I cast a glance at the retreating grindylows before swimming away. I hadn't got the feeling they were trying to trick me. I turned my attention back to Jeremy and had to increase my speed to keep up with him.

Even though we were swimming into the depths of the sea, the sun's rays still made their way through the water and lit up everything around us. I was thankful for that as I didn't fancy swimming through dark waters.

Jeremy stopped swimming and pointed to the structure in front of us.

I gasped. It was a real palace. A real sunken palace. It was made of white marble columns and a marble roof. It looked like an old Greek palace. There were elaborate steps surrounding it and many sea creatures had taken up residence on the steps.

I said to Jeremy, "How did this get down here?"

"I'm not sure. It's been here for thousands of years, just like the merpeople have. Let's go inside."

We swam between the columns and came to an open room. I spotted a huge, white chair at the back of the room on a small, marble platform. A merman was sitting in the chair and staring silently into the distance. As we got closer, I saw his resemblance to Nerita and Conway in his facial features. The merman had long, flowing hair which matched his long beard which moved gently on the sea's currents. There was an immense sadness in his eyes.

He looked our way and raised a hand slowly in greeting. "Cassia Winter? Is that you? Come closer. I thought for a second you were Rosalyn. You look so like her." He let out a heavy sigh. "You know the pain of losing someone, and now, so do I."

I swam over to King Taron and settled on the floor in front of him. I moved my hands gently at my side to stop myself from floating away.

I said, "I'm so sorry about Nerita. I will find out what happened to her." I paused before adding, "If she was murdered, I'll find the murderer."

King Taron gave me a slow nod. "I know you will. I have every faith in your abilities as a justice witch. I was good friends with Rosalyn. We shared many good swims together. I'm glad you've come to see me. I haven't been up to the surface of the sea for years. I'm not strong enough to do so these days." He sighed again. "I'm not strong enough to do much now. I was getting ready to hand my royal responsibilities over to Nerita."

"Will Conway take over now?" I asked.

"He'll have to. However, I don't think he's quite ready to do that." King Taron gave me a wry smile. "But I think his betrothed is ready. Have you met Isla yet?"

"I have. I hope you don't mind me asking you questions so soon after your loss, but I'd like to get on with my investigation quickly. Can I ask how you get on with Isla, please?"

"Well enough," King Taron said. "I like ambition in a mermaid and Isla has more than her fair share of it. Nerita also had ambition and often clashed with Isla. I suppose you're going to ask me if Nerita had any enemies."

I nodded. "I've already heard that she upset your people by the way she spoke to them."

King Taron let out a short laugh. "She did! She was abrupt, that's for sure. But she got results. She was a wonderful organiser. Once she set her mind on something, she'd see it through to the end. Our community was the most important thing in her life. She was extremely protective of our people and would go out of her way to keep everyone safe."

"What do you mean by that?" I asked.

"There are other merpeople communities out there who are jealous of our Brimstone way of life. Nerita has seen a couple of their leaders getting too close to our borders now and again. She had fierce words with them and warned them off. I suspect those same leaders were bothering her again recently because Nerita kept disappearing for hours on end these last few weeks. When I asked her about it, she said it was nothing important, and that she was dealing with it." He hesitated before continuing, "I know about the sirens disappearing. Nerita tried to keep that from me, but I've been king for a long time and I have many loyal subjects. One of the older vampire squids told me about their disappearance last week. I was waiting to get Nerita on her own to talk to her about the sirens. Alas, I didn't get the chance."

I asked, "What do you know about the sirens disappearing?"

King Taron gave me a long look before answering, "Nerita had something to do with their disappearance. A week ago, I overheard her talking to the leader of the sirens about a mission in another land. I thought she was getting ready to go into battle with another community of merpeople. I asked her about it afterwards, but she said I must have misheard her and that she had no plans to go into battle with anyone or to enter another land. I knew she was lying, but I couldn't get her to admit the truth."

"Do you think someone from another community could have caused her harm?"

"It's possible. She made many enemies with the other communities." He sighed heavily. "It's possible one of the leaders wanted Nerita out of the way for some reason. What that reason was, I don't know."

"How would I find out more information about her involvement with them?" I said.

"You should talk to Isla. She had a knack for knowing exactly what Nerita was up to. I think she often followed Nerita as she went about her duties. Cassia, be careful. Ambitious merpeople can be ruthless."

Chapter 11

We stayed with King Taron a while longer as he wanted to talk about Mum and the adventures they'd been on together. I was more than happy to listen to him and my knowledge of Mum grew even more. It made me feel warm and happy inside. I knew that I hadn't been ready to talk about her before, but now I wanted to know everything I could about her.

Before we left, I did my best to reassure King Taron that I'd find the creature responsible for Nerita's death.

He gave me a sad smile and said, "I know you will, Cassia, I know you will."

When we returned to the beach, I used magic to dry myself. I didn't want to blow my own trumpet, but I was pleased with how well it worked and I was completely dry within a minute. I reckoned that if I used my powers after a shower at home, I could do away with towels altogether.

Jeremy attempted to use his magic to dry himself but somehow ended up giving himself an electric shock. With his permission, I directed my hot air hands at him.

We headed over to the café and found Stanley fast asleep on a cushion behind the counter. Gia told us he'd fallen asleep soon after she'd fed him. I quickly told Gia about our talk with King Taron.

Gia looked around the café before taking us to one side. She said, "I wasn't sure whether to tell you this earlier, but I think it could be relevant to your investigation. Isla has been engaged to other mermen from different communities. From what I've heard, she goes for those mermen in a position of power in the hope of sharing that power."

"What happened to the other engagements?" I asked.

"The merman broke it off with her. Apparently, they got fed up of her controlling ways and her lust for power. She's been engaged to Conway for three months now, and he seems happy enough about the situation." She considered her words. "Perhaps compliant would be a better way of describing him. I think Conway likes Isla to make the decisions in their relationship. Now that he's going to take over from Nerita, I dread to think what Isla's going to be like around here. She's already asked me for a so-called royal discount on my goods."

Jeremy asked, "How many times has she been engaged?"

"Three times, that I've heard of."

Jeremy continued, "And which communities are these? Do they back onto the border of the Brimstone waters?"

Gia's eyes widened. "They do. You don't think Isla and her former boyfriends have something to do with Nerita's death, do you?"

Jeremy gave her a slow nod. "I've met some of the merpeople in the other communities. Some of them have an intense hate for Brimstone and its inhabitants. Isla could have convinced one of her exes to do away with Nerita so that she could come into power here. Perhaps she's going to give her partner in crime a piece of Brimstone in return."

Following Jeremy's logic, I said, "What if Nerita found out about Isla's plans? She could have gathered the sirens together to fight them. The sirens could be at war with another community right now."

Gia looked nervously towards the sea. "What if the sirens have been taken prisoner or worse? What if another community of merpeople are on their way here to attack us right now?"

Jeremy said, "That can't happen. There's a protective spell around the borders of Brimstone. Cassia's mum put it there years ago. I check it every week to make sure it's still working. I actually checked it earlier this morning. Everything is in order."

Gia gave him a small smile. "That's a relief. But where have the sirens gone? And are they okay?" She turned her expectant face to me. "Cassia, what are you going to do about this?"

I was saved from answering that difficult question by the arrival of a green Brimstone butterfly. It headed towards me and I knew it had a message for me. I opened my palm and it landed softly there.

Some butterfly messages are written on the wings of the creature, and some messages are vocal. This message was a vocal one - a very loud one.

Rex's voice boomed out, 'Cassia! This is Rex. We met earlier. I found one of the sirens on the other side of the Brimstone border. I ordered her to tell me where the rest of the sirens were. She refused and then began to sing one of her evil songs which made me and my colleagues fall asleep. When we came round, the siren had gone. We will not be put off that easily, we will continue to search for the sirens! End of message!'

Stanley woke up, yowled and jumped off his cushion. He looked left and right. "What's happening? Who's shouting? What's going on?"

I explained, "It was a butterfly message from Rex." I turned to the butterfly and gave it a reply for Rex. I told him I would await further details from him.

As the butterfly flew away, a yellow butterfly came in and alighted on my shoulder. The message was from Dr Morgan this time:

'Cassia, I've examined that water bottle and it is pure water. I won't go into details, but I've checked the corpse and found the pure water to be her cause of death as it turned her into her tailed self and stopped her from being able to breathe. I'd put the time of death between 11:30 and midday. I'll give you a full report later." Her tone turned indignant. "I haven't heard a word from Blythe or your gran since they went missing. I'm furious with the pair of them! And as for that useless guardian, Luca, I asked him where you were an hour ago and he yelled that he didn't know and he didn't care. Then he stormed away from me without a word of explanation. How rude! I don't know what's got into the residents around here lately. No one has any good manners left. Anyway, I'll catch you later. Bye for now.'

I sent a message to Dr Morgan and thanked her for her findings. I'd speak to the doctor later about Luca and his change towards me.

As the yellow butterfly left the café, a haunting tune came to us on a breeze. It sent shivers up and down my spine.

I said to Gia, "What's that?"

She pointed to the sea and the line of merpeople who were standing there looking out to the horizon. She said, "It's a mourning song. They're singing it for Nerita. It'll last for hours."

Stanley whimpered and padded over to me. He said, "Cassia, I don't like it. It's making my heart hurt."

I picked him up. "It's making mine hurt too. I don't think there's anything else we can do here at the moment. I'm not going to disturb the merpeople in their time of grief. Let's go back to the apartment."

We said goodbye to Gia, got onto our broomsticks and flew away from the sad scene. The desolate tune followed us for the next few miles and I couldn't stop the tears from rolling down my cheeks.

Chapter 12

As we flew back to Brimstone, I said to Jeremy, "You are welcome to stay at Gran's apartment tonight. I think the sofa pulls out into a bed."

Jeremy replied, "That's kind of you, but I've already booked myself into The Brimstone Hotel. I did that this morning before I turned up at Blythe's house. I had a feeling I'd be staying in Brimstone for a while. Staying at the hotel will give me a good opportunity to speak to the other guests about the merpeople and related matters."

I nodded. "That's a good idea. You can come over for dinner if you like? I'm sure Gilda has put something delicious in the fridge for us. She has a knack for knowing when we'll be staying at the apartment and always fills the fridge for us."

"As tempted as I am by that offer, I shall decline. I'd like to get on with my discreet interrogation of the hotel guests." He smiled. "And there's an all-you-can-eat buffet on tonight in the hotel's dining room. I don't think the manager knows what he's let himself in for with me on that score!"

Brimstone town came into view. Jeremy said goodbye to us and aimed his broomstick towards The Brimstone Hotel. He said he'd give us a full report of his findings in the morning.

The sky was turning a darker blue and a tiredness was settling on me. I mentally brushed it away. I didn't have time to be tired.

Instead of landing outside the apartment, I landed in front of Gran's cellar door.

I said to Stanley, "Let's have a quick check on Oliver. I want to make sure he's okay. He hides it well, but I know he's worried about Gran."

Stanley nodded. "Good idea. If he's very worried, shall we stay at Gran's house tonight instead of the apartment?"

"Absolutely."

I opened the cellar door and found Oliver curled up a few feet away from the door. His little body was rising and falling and I heard a quiet snore coming from him. I didn't want to wake him up so I quietly began to close the door.

Oliver immediately jumped to his paws and cried out, "Esther? Is that you?" He blinked as he focused his attention on us.

I stepped into the cellar with Stanley at my side. "Sorry, Oliver, it's only us. We wanted to see how you were doing."

Oliver's head dropped slightly. "I thought you were Esther coming back. Have you heard anything about her? Has anyone found her yet? Is anyone looking for her?"

I put my broomstick down and sat at Oliver's side. I said softly, "Some of the season witches are looking for Gran and Blythe. I met Jeremy Spring, and he told me the other season witches are out right now searching for them. He's confident that Gran and Blythe will be found soon." I was tempted to stroke Oliver's head, but he didn't normally allow me to do that. The few times I'd tried, he'd given me a disgusted look and then said he needed to wash himself. Instead, I said, "Oliver, have you had anything to eat?"

"I'm not hungry. What have you been up to in Brimstone? Why have you been talking to Jeremy Spring? Does he still look young?"

"He's told me a lot about Mum, and how he used to help her."

Stanley came to sit at Oliver's side, and between us, we told Oliver about our latest investigation.

Oliver listened intently and I was glad his mind had been taken off Gran for a while.

When we'd finished, he said, "I'm not familiar with the creatures of the sea. I've never been to the beach. From what I've seen on TV, there's too much water at the beach." He gave Stanley a kind look. "And I don't think

I'll ever go. I don't want to meet those horrible grindylows that attacked you. Are you sure you're okay now?"

Stanley nodded and said cheerfully, "I'm fine. It was quite an adventure. I knew Cassia would rescue me. She always looks out for me."

Oliver threw me one of his disgusted looks. "But it wasn't you who rescued Stanley, was it? You need to keep a closer eye on my brother, young lady."

Even though I was glad to see Oliver was back to his normal self, I didn't appreciate the telling-off. However, I remained silent and gave Oliver a nod of contrition.

Oliver continued, "Find out what you can about the sea creatures. I believe there are some books in Esther's apartment about them. Go back there now and see what you can turn up."

Stanley said, "We were going to stay here with you tonight to keep you company."

Oliver raised his furry chin. "I'm perfectly happy with my own company, but thank you anyway. Now that the season witches are on Esther's trail, I feel confident that she'll be back home very soon. I must tidy up before she returns. I haven't done a lick of housework since she left. I can't have her coming back to a mess." He nodded to himself. "I'll start on the upstairs first."

"Can we give you a hand?" I offered.

Oliver looked me over. "No, you'll be more of a hindrance than a help. Don't sit there on the floor looking useless; get yourselves back to Brimstone." He added a tut.

Stanley chucked. "Oliver, I love it when you're bossy. You're funny."

Oliver moved closer to Stanley and rubbed his cheek against his. His voice was a bit gruffer as he said, "Take good care of yourself, Stanley. Don't put yourself in any danger. And don't let Cassia put you in any danger either."

I said indignantly, "I never mean to put Stanley in danger. Things just happen sometimes."

Oliver pursed his lips at my words. I didn't even know cats could do that.

I got to my feet, picked up my broomstick and said, "Right, we'll see you later."

"Bye," Oliver said. "You know where the door is." He gave Stanley a smile before heading towards the cellar steps.

I shook my head at his departure. He was certainly back to his normal self.

Stanley and I headed straight back to the apartment. Once there, I checked the fridge and found a lasagne. I popped it in the oven and then gave Stanley a dish of something that immediately made him drool.

While the lasagne was warming up, we located the books on the sea creatures of Brimstone. There were only a few books and it wasn't going to take us long to go through them. I took them over to the sofa and sat down. Stanley sat on my knee and I read out the relevant paragraphs to him.

Stanley said, "There isn't a lot of information about the merpeople, is there? I thought there might be something on the different communities, and perhaps something on King Taron and his family."

I placed the book I'd just been reading on the table in front of me. "Perhaps Gran never dealt with the sea creatures and so didn't need to know a lot about them. From what Jeremy said, it was Mum who kept an eye on the activities at Brimstone Beach. I wonder if she ever kept any records of her work there? I'll ask Jeremy about that tomorrow."

The oven pinged to notify me the lasagne was ready. Stanley had kindly offered to wait until my meal was ready before he had his.

We took our food over to the table and looked out at the town of Brimstone as we ate.

I noted, "Everyone looks happy out there. I can't see any signs of trouble, can you?"

With his cheeks bulging with food, Stanley said, "Nope. But it could be the calm before the storm."

I waved my empty fork at the citizens of Brimstone and said to them, "If anyone is thinking of committing a murder, would you mind waiting until I've finished my present investigation, please? Thank you. I appreciate your patience." I stuck my fork into the lasagne and scooped a portion of the delicious meal into my mouth. I don't know what Gilda did to her food, but it always tasted amazing. I gave the lasagne my full attention and soon had an empty plate.

I leant back in my chair and patted my happy stomach. Gilda had also left some tiramisu in the fridge. I'd wait a while before I attacked that.

I said, "Stanley, I think we should talk to Conway's girlfriend first thing tomorrow. What do you think?"

Stanley's eyes were closing. He muttered, "Good idea. I think I'll close my eyes for a while. They feel very heavy. But you keep talking; I'm listening."

I smiled at my tired friend. "It's time for your sleep. Come on, little one." I picked him up and took him into the bedroom. I placed him on the large, comfy cushion at the side of my bed. Stanley was asleep before I'd even settled him down. I stroked his head and whispered 'goodnight' and then returned to the living area.

I looked out of the window and noticed Luca walking around the town square with his hands clasped behind his back. Many residents nodded and smiled at him as they passed by, but Luca only gave them a tight smile in return. When I'd seen him making his rounds of the town before, he would stop and chat with everyone he met, and he laughed and smiled constantly as he did so. What had Astrid done to him to make him so miserable now?

Placing my hand against the glass, I said quietly, "Luca, when this investigation is over, I'm going to do all that I can to help you. I promise."

I turned away from the window and took my empty plate and Stanley's empty bowl over to the sink. I just had enough room in my stomach to fit in the tiramisu. As expected, the mixture of cream, soft sponge and the light taste of coffee was delicious.

With a full stomach and a sleeping cat at my side, I settled into my bed and it didn't take me long to fall into a deep sleep.

As soon as I woke up in the morning, my senses sprang into high alert. There was something different about the apartment.

Chapter 13

I looked over at Stanley who was standing on his cushion and sniffing loudly. He looked at me and said, "There's a funny smell. Can you smell it?"

I pulled myself into a seated position. "I can. It smells like the sea. How is that possible? The beach is ten miles away."

Stanley's whiskers twitched. "Someone has been in this apartment. They've left that smell behind. The intruder might still be here. I'm going to investigate." He made a move forward.

"Wait!" I hissed. "If there is an intruder out there, they could be armed and dangerous. Let me find some sort of weapon first." I pulled the bedcover back, got out of bed and started to look left and right.

Stanley whispered, "Cassia, you're armed and dangerous already! You don't need weapons. You've got your magic. Use it."

I looked down at my hands. "Oh, yeah. I keep forgetting." I held my hands out in front of me in what I hoped was a menacing manner and walked towards the door. "Stanley, stay behind me. I'll go first."

Bracing myself, I opened the door and stepped through it. I headed towards the living area, my hands held aloft ready for action.

It took me all of ten seconds to realise no one was there. My nose wrinkled. The smell was stronger here. It was a mixture of the sea, hot sand and a hint of cooked food.

Stanley made his way around the apartment with his nose to the floor. When he'd completed a circuit, he returned to my side and announced, "Whoever was here has gone now. I examined the door and couldn't find any signs of forced entry. Also, I can't see that anything is missing or has been disturbed." He gave me a little grin. "I sound very professional, don't I?"

"You do." I put my hands on my hips and looked around again. "Why would someone come in and not take anything?"

Stanley didn't answer. He was staring at something under the table near the window.

"What's wrong?" I asked him. "Have you seen a mouse?"

Stanley padded over to the table, went under it and came out with something in his mouth. He dropped it at my feet.

I picked it up. "It's a hair comb. A sparkly hair comb. It looks just like the one that Isla was wearing." I looked down at Stanley. "Does this mean Isla was our intruder? Why? What did she want?"

"The obvious answer is that she's the one who murdered Nerita and doesn't want you to find out. She must have sneaked into our apartment last night and ..." he trailed off.

"Had a good look around, left her comb and then cleared off?" I suggested. "That doesn't make sense."

"Or," Stanley held up a paw, "someone else could have left this comb here as a message for us. They must have known I'd find it under the table. Someone from the beach must have seen me searching for shells and realised what an inquisitive cat I am." He gave me a satisfied nod. "I am very nosy. Just like you."

"Nosiness is a virtue," I told him. I turned the comb over in my hands. "Do you think the message is for us to keep an eye on Isla? If so, someone at the beach must suspect her of something. They didn't need to leave us a message; she's already on my list of suspects. Having this comb in the apartment gives me the perfect excuse to speak to her." I looked at the comb again. "It's beautiful. I wonder what those stones are?"

I jumped as someone knocked on the door.

Before I could respond, Stanley ran over to the door and popped his head through the cat flap. A second later, he pulled his head back through and announced, "It's Jeremy!"

"Stanley, you shouldn't have stuck your head out like that! It could have been the murderer out there." I tried to give him a hard look, but it was impossible to do as he was so cute.

Stanley lowered his head a bit. "Sorry. I won't do it again."

I gave him a quick pat on the head to show him I wasn't mad before opening the door.

"Morning!" Jeremy trilled holding out a cardboard cup to me. "I've brought hot tea straight from the café. Gilda assures me it will wake you up in a second." Was it my imagination or did he look even younger this morning?

I took the cup and opened the door wider to allow him to enter. "Thank you. Would you like a drink? I can put the kettle on."

"No, thank you. I've had a full breakfast at the café this morning." Jeremy smiled down at Stanley. "Hello there, friend. How are you?" He abruptly stopped talking and raised his head. His nostrils flared. "Why does it smell like Brimstone Beach in here?"

I gave Jeremy the comb and told him our thoughts about who might have left it here.

Jeremy examined the comb. There was annoyance in his eyes. "I don't like the idea of someone coming into your apartment while you are asleep. How dare they?" He handed the comb back to me and closed the door behind us. He held his hands out towards the door. "I'm putting a spell on this useless piece of wood to stop any supernatural creatures coming in without your permission."

Flashes of green light shot from Jeremy's fingers and landed on the door like little exploding fireworks. I was worried for a moment that the door was going to burst into flames.

Jeremy wriggled his fingers and the green light disappeared. "That will do it. The only way supernatural creatures can get through that door is if you invite them in. The nerve of some creatures!"

"There was no harm done," I told him. "Come and sit down on the sofa. I want to hear all about your night at the hotel. Did you find out anything useful?"

Jeremy gave the door an annoyed look before following Stanley and me over to the sofa. I sat at one end and Stanley sat at my side. As soon as Jeremy took a seat, Stanley moved onto his lap and looked up at him with wide eyes. He looked impossibly cute.

Jeremy immediately fell under Stanley's spell and a smile spread across his face. He began to stroke Stanley and all the anger over the intruder left his face. Stanley had a calming effect on most beings.

I took a sip of the tea and felt a shot of caffeine zinging through my body. It felt like I'd plugged myself into a charger.

Jeremy began, "Let me begin by saying that you and Stanley have a lot of support in this town. The residents have nothing but praise for you and all the work you've done here. They know how difficult things are for you at present with Blythe and Esther gone, and many of them have offered their assistance to you, if you need it." His smile grew. "This really is a lovely town."

"Apart from the murderers out there," Stanley said.

Jeremy nodded. "Apart from the murderers. Speaking of which, I did some digging on Isla and I spoke to a sand-elf who used to live near a beach in another town. This was early last year and he recalls that Isla lived in that area too. He said it was hard to forget her as she was so loud and bossy! Anyway, she was engaged to a prince but then he broke the engagement off."

I nodded. "That's what Gia told us. This is good tea." I took another sip and felt my brain notching up a gear. "I can tell by your expression that you've got more to tell us about that engagement."

"I have. After the prince broke off the engagement, Isla tried to make light of the situation and told everyone she was fine about it. But then the prince suffered a terrible accident a few days later. A pile of underwater rocks fell on him whilst he was asleep." He paused for effect. "He was almost killed. Isla had been spotted at the very same pile of rocks the previous day by a family of starfish. She denied it and said she wouldn't stay with a community of merpeople who thought she was capable of such a terrible act. She left that area and arrived at Brimstone."

I gave Jeremy a thoughtful look. "So the message of your story is to be careful around Isla."

"Definitely. The sand-elf went on to say that he saw Isla leaving that day. She looked furious and there was such an intense hate in her eyes that the sand-elf fled the beach in terror. He only returned when Isla had gone. He heard the other merpeople saying how glad they were that Isla had gone. No one liked her."

"I'll speak to her about her previous engagements," I said. "I wonder if her thirst for power caused her to kill Nerita? As the pure water that killed Nerita is dangerous to merpeople, perhaps she forced another sea creature to get it for her." My brain cells were working harder. "And when she had that bottle of water, she must have lured Nerita into the cave and then tricked her into drinking it." My attention went to the comb at my side. "Jeremy, would it be possible for a merperson to walk all the way to this apartment? If Isla or another merperson left this here, how did they do it? Wouldn't they be in immense pain?"

"They would. The further they go from the sea on legs, the more painful it becomes for them. They could have used a different form of transport. I could ask the flying unicorns if they've had any merpeople using their taxi services recently."

"Thank you. What about the sirens? Would one of them be able to get here easily?"

"Yes, I suppose they would. Do you think one of the missing sirens came here specially to give you that comb as a warning against Isla?"

I nodded. "It's a possibility. I'm not ruling anything out." I drained the last of my tea. "As soon as I've had my breakfast and got dressed, I'm going back to the beach to talk to Isla. I have many questions for her. Jeremy, are you coming with us?"

"I won't. I'll stay here and continue asking questions around town about the merpeople. Someone may have seen the creature who came into this apartment." His face twisted in disgust. "I hope someone did see them. I want to know who it was."

I put my hand on his arm. "Don't get upset about that. Nothing's been stolen and nothing has been damaged."

"I'm not bothered about property damage and theft," Jeremy said. His eyes welled up. "What if something terrible had happened to you? I couldn't bear that. I feel responsible for you."

I squeezed his arm and gave him a bright smile. "You don't need to. I can look after myself."

Stanley turned his face to Jeremy and added, "And I can look after Cassia. We'll be fine. Just fine."

Chapter 14

Stanley and I flew back to Brimstone Beach. I saw merpeople sitting and lying on the sand, quietly talking to each other. No one was playing any games, and no one was laughing.

We landed outside the café and found Gia wiping down a table. She raised her hand in acknowledgement.

When we went over to her, she said, "It's been a very quiet morning. I haven't had anyone buy any water bottles from me." Concern came into her eyes. "I hope the merpeople don't think I had anything to do with Nerita's death."

"I'm sure they don't think that." I glanced towards the sea water bottles behind the counter. "How long have those bottles been there?"

"About an hour. I put the ones that had been there yesterday in a locked cabinet in case you needed them. I've been thinking about the poisoned water. What if Nerita wasn't the intended victim? What if someone just wanted any merperson to die and didn't care who? What if someone is planning on killing the merpeople population one by one?" She twisted the cloth in her hands and her face lost its remaining colour. "How far have you got with your investigation? Do you have any suspects yet?"

"I do. Gia, please try not to worry. Things will get sorted out. I won't stop until I find out who killed Nerita." I looked towards the merpeople on the sand. "Do you know where Isla is? I'd like to speak to her."

Gia raised her cloth towards the sea. "She's out there, near Turtle Island. I did see her on the sand a short while ago but she got fed up with how quiet everyone is and said she was going for a swim. I don't think she understands the concept of grief. Cassia, is there anything I can do to help you with your investigation?"

There was no way I was putting Gia's life in danger so I said, "No, thank you. But if you do hear anything that might help me, you can let me know."

Gia continued to twist the cloth. "Of course."

I looked at the small island in the distance. "How do I get to Turtle Island? Can I swim there? I'm not the best swimmer, but I think I can make it."

"You could fly there," Gia suggested. "It's safe to land on Turtle Island. You won't find any wild animals there."

Stanley nudged into my leg. "Let's fly there. I've never been on an island before."

"Are you sure? You can stay here with Gia and I'll go."

"I want to go. As long as we keep away from the water's edge, I'll be fine." Stanley bared his little teeth in a brave smile.

"Okay. Come on."

We said goodbye to Gia and then flew over to the small island. It was a rough, round shape and was no bigger than thirty feet in diameter. As we got nearer, I could see Isla swimming around Turtle Island with an annoyed look on her beautiful face. Her lips were moving and it looked like she was muttering to herself. She wasn't wearing her hair comb. Did that mean the one I'd found in the apartment was hers?

I managed to land in the middle of the island. It had a smooth surface with small ridges here and there. There wasn't any vegetation on it but I did see a few crabs scuttling around.

Stanley sat down where we landed and looked nervously at the sea. "I think I'll stay right here if that's okay with you?"

"Of course it is." I looked right as Isla swam past the edge of the island, her tail flapping furiously behind her. "You'll probably be able to hear everything I say to Isla from here. If she slows down long enough for me to get her attention, that is."

I moved to the edge of the island and noticed there wasn't any sand there, just more of the smooth, slightly ridged material that I was standing on. I called out Isla's name as she swam nearer. She either didn't hear me or chose to ignore me. Either way, she didn't stop and continued her furious swim while mumbling to herself.

I moved a little closer to the water, put a hand to the side of my mouth and yelled, "Isla! I want to talk to you right now!"

Isla's head shot my way as she came closer. Annoyance crossed her features and she shouted, "What do you want? Can't you see I'm busy?"

She dipped under the water and zoomed by me without stopping. Her tail flipped upwards and then hit the sea with a huge splash which sent a wave washing over me. I heard a yelp behind me and saw a puddle of water rushing towards Stanley. I raced over to his side and picked him up. I waited until the water trickled away from us and then put Stanley down.

He said, "Why won't she stop and talk to you? She keeps swimming round and round. She's going to make herself very dizzy soon."

"I don't have time for her nonsense." I quickly used my magic hot air fingers to dry myself and then marched back to the edge of the island. As Isla approached, I raised my hands and performed an immobilising spell on the mermaid. I'd never used it in water before and I didn't know whether it would work.

It did work.

Isla face was frozen in shock as she floated helplessly on the current towards me. I knelt down, reached out and grabbed her by the shoulder. I pulled her close and used my free hand to wipe the magic from her ears. I wanted her to hear me.

"Isla, I'm here to talk to you about my investigation. I've got many questions for you and you are going to answer them. Now, I can keep you in this suspended state while I do so, or I can set you free on the proviso that you don't swim away until I finish asking my questions. Which is it to be?" I cleared the magic from her mouth so she could talk.

She spat out, "How dare you do this to me? Set me free immediately. I'll make sure King Taron knows about this. He'll be furious."

"He won't. I spoke to him yesterday, and he wants me to find out what happened to Nerita." I still had one hand on her shoulder as I didn't want her bobbing away. "You know that I'm a justice witch and that I have certain powers in this area. I am more than happy to keep you in this frozen state for a while."

Isla's lips tightened in annoyance. If her eyes had been able to narrow in hate, I'm sure they would have.

"Alright," she said with a sigh. "I promise not to swim away until I've answered your questions. I'm not happy about it, though."

"Your happiness is not my concern. If you make any attempts to swim away, I will use my magic on you again." I didn't like being so harsh, but sometimes it was needed. I waved my hands over Isla and removed the immobilising spell. She wiggled her shoulders and her tail flapped angrily in the water behind her.

I began with, "Nerita died between 11.30 and midday yesterday. Where were you at that time, and do you have any witnesses to confirm that?"

She raised her hand and moved it around her. "I was here, swimming. As for witnesses, I prefer to be alone. But I'm sure if you ask some of the other mermaids, one of them would have seen me. The younger ones are always looking at me. They admire me. I can see it in their faces."

"That's not ideal, but I'll speak to the other mermaids about you. What was your relationship like with Nerita?"

Isla rolled her eyes. "I've already made it clear how I felt about her. I didn't like her, and she didn't like me. Conway should have been the one with the royal responsibilities,

79

not her. He's much better with our people than Nerita was. He's much more compassionate and understanding. Just like me. As soon as this silly mourning business is over, we can get married and start ruling this area in the way it should be ruled. How many more questions have you got?"

I ignored her last comment and said, "I've been told about your previous engagements, and about a prince who was hurt in suspicious circumstances."

Isla came closer to me and rested her arms on the edge of the island. Her direct gaze was unnerving. She said, "Idle gossip. I didn't think justice witches were supposed to pay attention to idle gossip. I thought you were supposed to concentrate on the facts."

I lifted my head. I was not going to be intimidated by her. "Have you been previously engaged?"

She gave me a slow nod. "I have. A few times. But not to the right merman. Conway is the right one for me."

"Did one of your former fiancés suffer injuries during an accident?"

Keeping her look steady, she replied, "I believe so. I wasn't there at the time of the accident. I was with some friends of mine when it happened. My friends told the prince's father that I was with them, but he didn't believe them. He never liked me and wanted to get rid of me from the day I became engaged to his son." One of her perfect eyebrows rose. "Aren't you going to ask me if I killed Nerita? I can see that you're thinking it."

"Did you?"

"No. As much as I disliked her, I wouldn't do that to Conway. I love him. Really love him."

I reached into my back pocket and took out the hair comb. I held it up and said, "Is this yours?"

Her other eyebrow rose now. One of her hands shot out in an attempt to grab the comb. I was ready for her and swiftly moved it out of the way.

"Hey!" she called in protest. "Where did you get that? It's mine."

"I found it in my apartment this morning. Did you put it there?"

"No! Someone must have stolen it from my cave last night. I've been looking for it all morning." Her eyes glistened with tears and she lowered her hand. "I thought I'd lost it, Please, can I have it back?"

I lowered the comb a fraction. "Who would steal it from you and then place it in my apartment?"

Isla sniffed and dashed away a tear. "Lots of merpeople. They're jealous of me. They want to get me into trouble. I swear that I had nothing to do with Nerita's death." She held her hand out. "Can I have it back? Please?"

I considered the matter and concluded there was no harm in giving the comb back to Isla. I handed it over. She said thank you and then swept her hair to one side and placed the sparkling comb there.

Isla said, "Have you spoken to Rex yet about Nerita?"

"Rex? We have talked about another matter concerning Nerita. Why are you asking me about Rex?"

"Rex was in a relationship with Nerita, but she ended it recently. He was heartbroken. Still is. You should talk to him about that. Have you got any more questions? I want to see how Conway is. He hasn't come up to the surface at all today. I hope he doesn't take too long to get over Nerita's death. I want to talk to him about our wedding plans."

Her matter-of-factness over Nerita's death rendered me speechless for a few seconds. I said, "I don't have any more questions for now."

Without hesitating, Isla dipped beneath the water and swam away. Her tail gave one last flap sending a small wave my way. I jumped out of its way.

The ground beneath me listed to the side and I thought for a second that I was falling over.

Stanley cried out in terror, "Cassia! The island is sinking! We're going to drown!"

Water gushed towards his paws.

Chapter 15

I raced over to Stanley and scooped him into my arms. I was about to fly us out of danger when a deep voice spoke.

"I do apologise. I didn't realise I had visitors. Come closer; let me see you."

Stanley's eyes were wide as he looked left and right. He whispered, "Who said that? Did you hear that? Tell me you heard it, otherwise I'll think I'm going mad."

"I did hear something." I looked left and right too but I couldn't see anyone.

The ground beneath us moved again and water ran over my feet.

"Over here, my friends," the voice said, "to your right and downwards."

We both looked that way and saw a huge turtle's face peering back at us. Wrinkles lined his face and his eyes twinkled with joy. "Is that you, Cassia Winter? Come closer, please. I'm not as young as I used to be and my eyes are not as sharp as they once were."

I whispered to Stanley, "Turtle Island! It's actually a turtle and not an island. Or is he a living island that's shaped like a turtle? Is Turtle his first name and Island his surname?"

Stanley whispered back, "I've no idea. Do you think it's safe to move closer? He looks friendly enough."

I stole another glance at the turtle's smiling face and decided it was safe to move closer.

I kept Stanley in my arms as I made my way towards his head. The ground, or rather, the turtle's back, kept moving gently from side to side. It was like being on a moving bus.

"Ah!" the turtle declared as we stopped near his head. "It is you, Cassia. How wonderful it is to meet you again. I don't suppose you remember meeting me when you were young? You used to visit me with your mum."

"I'm sorry, I don't remember that at all. And I'm sorry for landing on your back and walking about."

The turtle chuckled. "I didn't feel a thing. I only realised you two were here when I heard you screaming just now. Was that my fault? Did I scare you? I didn't mean to, but it's time for me to submerge myself and return to the bottom of the sea for a while. If I'd have known you were on my back, I would have stayed still."

Stanley said, "You did scare me a bit, but that's because I'm frightened of the sea."

The turtle gave him a slow nod. "That's understandable." He tilted his big head to one side and his twinkling eyes narrowed a fraction. "Cassia, are you here to investigate the death of that young mermaid?"

I nodded. "I am. I don't suppose you know anything about it, do you?"

"No, I'm afraid not. I tend to keep to myself. I've been in these waters for more years than I care to remember and I've realised that the cause of most problems around here is love. Creatures change when they're in love. They lose their common sense. Don't you find that, Cassia?"

"I suppose so. I've just discovered that Nerita was in a relationship with someone, so love could be a factor in Nerita's death."

"Indeed." The turtle turned his head and gazed out to the horizon. "Love is supposed to be a magical thing, but it often leads to tragedy." He glanced back at us. "While I would like to chat to you some more, I really must go under the water. My back is beginning to sting under this sun."

"Oh! Right. Yes. Sorry, we didn't mean to keep you." I smiled at the turtle. "It's been lovely to talk to you."

"You too, Cassia Winter." He cast me a slow smile. "You're so like your mother. I'll wait until you're safely on your broomstick before submerging. Goodbye for now. Good luck with your investigation. Remember to look for the love as you go along."

Stanley waved his paw in farewell and then got onto my broomstick with me. We moved off the turtle's back and watched as he slowly sank beneath the sea.

Stanley said, "What a magnificent creature."

"He is. I think he's given me some good advice about looking for the love in this case. Rex never mentioned his involvement with Nerita when we first spoke to him. I think it's time to talk to him again." I scanned the sea below us. "Where will we find him?"

"Would you mind if we returned to dry land for a while? I don't like to be near so much water."

I looked down at my little friend and noticed he was trembling. "Oh, Stanley, I didn't realise. Sorry. I'll take us back to the café. And I'll get you something to eat."

As we headed back to the beach, something caught my eye in the waters below. I looked down and saw a couple of grindylows on the surface of the water. They were waving their thin green arms our way and staring up at us. They were saying something but I couldn't make it out from this distance.

I put my hand on Stanley's back and said, "Don't panic, but I'm going closer to those grindylows for a moment. I think they want to tell me something."

Stanley's back arched beneath my hand. He hissed, "Don't let them get me! I don't want to play with them!"

"I won't let anything happen to you," I promised.

I swooped lower and went closer to the grindylows. Their green faces beamed up at me.

In a childlike voice, one of them said, "We have to talk to you! We know a secret! We know a secret about the dead mermaid! We have to tell you!" He ended this with a giggle and waved his hands at us to beckon us closer.

Stanley shivered and said, "It's a trick! Don't fall for it."

"I don't think it is a trick," I replied. "Stanley, I'll take you back to the café and then I'll come back here and talk to the grindylows." I waved down to the green-faced creatures and called out, "I'll be back in a few minutes."

I flew over to the café and ignored Stanley's warnings about going anywhere near the grindylows. He was convinced they intended to drag me down to the depths of the ocean and keep me there.

As I placed Stanley in Gia's welcoming arms a short while later, I said to him, "The grindylows won't hurt me. Don't forget that I'm a witch. I can use my magic if I get into trouble." I kissed the top of his head. "Trust me."

Stanley didn't look convinced and Gia tried to take his mind off my visit to the green creatures by offering him a sardine lollipop. I ignored Stanley's worried face as I hurried out of the café.

As I walked along the sand towards the water, I tried to recall the words Jeremy had muttered yesterday, the ones for the spell that allowed us to breathe under water. There was only way I was going to find out if I remembered the correct words. I stopped at the water's edge and looked out.

The grindylows were bobbing in the sea a short distance ahead of me and kept beckoning me closer. They had such cheeky smiles on their faces and looked like mischievous children who were up to no good.

I recited the words of the spell and then stepped cautiously into the water. When I was in deep enough, I slowly dipped my head under the water and attempted to breathe. I was half expecting water to rush up my nose. But that didn't happen. I had performed the spell correctly. A twinge of smugness passed through me, then I remembered why I was doing this.

I ducked fully under the water and headed for the small, green creatures. They were waiting beneath the water now and curled their fingers towards themselves in a 'come closer' motion. There was mischief in their eyes and big smiles on their faces. I felt a flicker of fear. Was I doing the right thing? Or was this a trick?

The grindylows turned their backs on me and began to swim away. One of them came back over to me and wrapped its thin fingers tightly around my arm. She giggled as she did so. For a little creature, she was strong and I felt myself being pulled helplessly downwards.

Just when I thought about using magic to free myself from the creature's grip, we came to a stop in front of an underwater cave.

The grindylow holding me said, "Mum wants to talk to you. She heard the dead mermaid talking to someone. She wants to tell you about it."

I looked towards the cave and expected an older version of the grindylows to come out. The creature who swam out was older, but not by much. She had the same childlike face and mischievous look in her eyes as the smaller creatures who were now swimming around my feet. She stopped in front of me and giggled.

"Hello," I said. "I believe you have some information for me about Nerita, the mermaid. Is that right?"

The mum grindylow put her hands over her mouth and giggled again. She lowered her hands and said, "Yes! I heard the dead mermaid. I heard her talking to those sirens. She was so bossy! So loud!" She put her hands back to her mouth and giggled some more. The other grindylows giggled too.

I said, "What did the mermaid say?"

She dropped her hands. "That bossy mermaid said the sirens had to do something for her, something important. She said they had to go into another world and be an army against some humans."

"Humans?" I felt my blood run cold. "Is that what she definitely said?"

The grindylow nodded. "She said they had to go into that world immediately and not tell anyone what they were doing. They couldn't tell King Taron. Oh no! She kept saying that over and over. 'Don't tell King Taron! I'm dealing with this! I'm in charge!' That's what she said. She told the sirens they had to be ready for the humans. They had to collect them. She said her uncle knows what they're doing, but her father doesn't."

"Her uncle?"

The grindylow nodded enthusiastically. "Yes. Her uncle knows about the humans, but the king doesn't. That's what the bossy mermaid said. I heard her."

"When did the mermaid talk to the sirens?" I asked.

The grindylow's face creased in thought. "Two days ago? Six days ago? Fifteen days ago? I can't remember. But the bossy mermaid told them to go and get those humans." The grindylow wagged a finger at me. "And don't tell King Taron! That's what she said. And then the sirens went. They've gone. All of them. And now, so has that bossy mermaid. She's gone forever."

"Did you hear anything else?" I asked.

The grindylow shook her head. A calculating look came into her eyes. "Come into our cave. You can play with us. You can stay here forever and play with us."

The other grindylows moved slowly towards me with eager expressions on their faces. I felt little fingers curling around my arms.

I shrugged myself free. "No, thank you. I have to go. Thank you for letting me know about Nerita and the sirens. Goodbye."

I shot off at a speed I didn't know I possessed. I didn't stop swimming until I reached the beach. Once I dried myself off using my amazing hot air hands, I strode towards the café to see Stanley's relieved face peering out at me. I was just as relieved as him to be back safely on dry land.

As I entered the café, Gia handed me a welcome cup of tea. I took it and asked her, "What do you know about Nerita's uncle."

"Nerita's uncle?" She gave me a slow nod. "Yes, I know plenty about him. You'd better sit down."

Chapter 16

I took my cup of tea over to a table at the front of the café and looked out onto the sea. I couldn't see any beings of any sort swimming about out there. Stanley settled himself on the chair at my side and asked me what the grindylows had said to me.

I waited for Gia to take a seat opposite us before telling them about my strange conversation.

Stanley said, "What do you think it all means? Why would Nerita send the sirens into the human world? What did she want them to do there?"

"Collect them, whatever that means," I answered. I looked at Gia. "Have any humans ever made their way into this area? Apart from me and other witches."

"Never. Why do you ask that?"

"I was wondering if some humans had become a threat to this area somehow. Perhaps Nerita discovered them and decided to put an end to any further trouble. Gia, how would the sirens get into the human world anyway? I have to go through Gran's door to return to my world. Are there any doors around here that the sirens could use?"

"I'm not sure about a door, but I do think there is a way into your world from here. I heard your mum talking about it once. Jeremy would know more about that, and so would Rex."

I nodded. "I need to speak to Rex about another matter, so I'll ask him about that too. Did you know he was in a relationship with Nerita?"

Gia's eyebrows shot up. "Was he? I didn't know that. It must have been a secret relationship. Who told you about it?"

"Isla did."

Gia gave me a knowing look. "Well, if there was something going on with Rex and Nerita, Isla would have known. She was always following Nerita around to see

89

what she was up to." She shook her head in disbelief. "Rex and Nerita? They seem an unlikely pair. But who am I to judge? Shall I tell you about Nerita's uncle now? I was surprised to hear you mention him. Mortimer hasn't been spoken about for years around here."

I cupped my tea in my hands and said, "Yes, I'd like to know all about him, please."

Gia began, "Mortimer is older than King Taron. He found this area years ago, led the merpeople here and then made himself king. He wasn't a fair or just king. He had a malicious streak. He liked to organise competitions and get the sea creatures to battle against each other. Mortimer organised these events just for his own pleasure. If a creature got hurt, it seemed to make him happier. His brother couldn't bear it and often pleaded with him to stop. Mortimer refused.

"Things came to a head one day when Mortimer ordered Nerita and Conway to fight each other." Gia's face twisted in disgust. "They were only young at the time, not much older than toddlers. Mortimer didn't have children of his own and he said whoever won the battle would become his heir. That was the breaking point for Taron. He refused to let his children fight each other and said he would take on Mortimer instead. Whoever won that fight would stay king forever. The other would be banished from this area and a spell would be cast on them which would make them lose their merman abilities. They would never be able to return to the sea."

I put my cup down. "It's obvious that King Taron won. But how? Did he have help? Was he injured in the fight?"

Gia gave me a sad smile. "His children's health and happiness were at stake and that gave Taron the strength to take on his older, and stronger, brother. I've heard tales about how the fight lasted for hours and how Taron never gave up even when he'd been beaten to a pulp. He kept going until he won the fight. Once he was king, Taron ordered his brother to leave the sea and never to return."

"Where is Mortimer now?" I asked.

Gia shrugged. "No one knows. I don't know if he's in Brimstone anymore. He could have moved to another town. I don't know why Nerita talked about her uncle to the sirens. She was only little when Mortimer left and I wouldn't have thought she'd remember him. Had she been in touch with him recently?" Her brow creased. "You could ask the guardians in town about his whereabouts. If Mortimer is living in the forest or on the outskirts of Brimstone, the guardians might know where he is. Isn't Luca the guardian who's in charge? You could ask him."

I shared a quick look with Stanley. I didn't want to talk to Luca in his present state. It hurt my heart too much.

Stanley placed his paw on my knee. "We can't ignore him forever, Cassia. Especially if he could help us with this investigation."

"You're right," I said with a small smile. "We have to talk to him." I looked back at Gia. "We'll go back to the town now and find Luca. If you see Rex, will you let him know I need to talk to him, please?"

"I will do."

I quickly finished my tea and we headed back to Brimstone town centre. From the air, we spotted Luca sitting on his own on the gazebo steps. His elbows were resting on his knees and his chin was in his hands. He was staring into the distance and looked forlorn. He looked so lost and alone.

We landed at the side of the gazebo and I let out a polite cough. Luca looked our way and lifted his chin from his hands. I'm not sure if I imagined it, but I could have sworn I saw a glimmer of recognition in his eyes. His lips lifted a minuscule amount at the corners as if he were about to smile.

That all changed in a second and that horrible cold look came into his eyes instead.

"What do you want?" he snapped.

"Your help," I replied as calmly as I could in the presence of his hate. "As a guardian, you have a duty to help me. I'm still dealing with the murder of Nerita and I've come across new information. I'd like to ask you something."

Luca's lips twisted in disgust and I felt my heart withering a touch. To have him look at me like that was breaking my heart. I felt my eyes stinging and quickly blinked. This was not the time to cry!

"What do you want to know? Make it quick."

I kept my eyes firmly fixed on his face. Out of the corner of my eye, I spotted Stanley moving slowly towards Luca's feet. He sat down and stared up at Luca's face with hope in his eyes.

I told Luca about my conversation with the grindylows, and then Gia. I ended with, "Do you know where Mortimer lives?"

I almost didn't get my last words out. During my conversation, Stanley had cheekily leant against Luca's legs. As if that wasn't shocking enough, Luca's hand had reached down and started to stroke Stanley's head. I don't think Luca was aware of what he was doing.

Luca said, "Yeah, I do know where he lives. I'll give you the directions. Are you going to talk to Mortimer now?" He continued to stroke Stanley.

"Yes. No time like the present." I let out a ridiculously high-pitched laugh out of nervousness. I was worried he'd register what he was doing to Stanley any second.

Luca gave me the directions to Mortimer's home and said, "Do you need me to accompany you?"

I was tempted to say yes, but I couldn't bear the thought of his icy looks for much longer. I was already feeling frostbite in my heart because of those looks. "No, thank you. I'll be fine."

"Well, you be careful out there. Mortimer isn't the most pleasant of people." He blinked as if surprised by his words. He cleared his throat and added, "I don't want to be collecting your dead body. I haven't got time for that."

"I'll do my best to stay alive." The stupid laugh erupted from me again. I sounded like a nervous hyena.

Stanley let out a little purr at Luca's feet. Luca jumped and looked down at him. He stared at the hand that was stroking Stanley and abruptly lifted it. He held it up and examined it as if not sure it belonged to him. He gave Stanley a half smile before swiftly getting to his feet.

Luca noisily cleared his throat again and muttered, "Let me know how you get on." He strode away without a backwards glance.

I pointed at Stanley. "You are a very brazen cat. You have no shame."

Stanley chuckled. "I know. I couldn't help myself. I had a sniff of Luca just then, and I caught a whiff of his old self. Our friend is still in there somewhere. I know his memories of us will come back soon. They have to." He paused. "His memories will come back, won't they?"

I sighed. "I honestly don't know. Let's not talk about Luca." I lowered my broomstick. "Come on; let's find the mysterious, and possibly dangerous, Uncle Mortimer."

Chapter 17

Of course, Mortimer lived in the darkest, deepest part of the forest in a cottage hidden from view. If Mortimer decided to attack us, there wouldn't be any helpful passers-by ready to leap to our defence.

We landed in front of the small, rundown cottage which belonged to Mortimer and looked around us nervously. The cottage was placed in a space between two, tall trees which blotted out the sun. One small ray was trying its best to shed light on the cottage roof. The dilapidated building was made of wood and the roof was sparsely thatched. The windows were grimy and covered in cobwebs. A sign on the rotting front door announced that visitors were not welcome and we should 'clear off if you know what's good for you!'

Stanley said, "Perhaps we should clear off. Or come back with Luca? I'm getting a bad feeling about this."

I waggled my free hand at him and said, "Don't you worry; I will perform magic if needed." My other hand was firmly clasped around my broomstick. I wanted to be ready to fly away immediately if necessary.

Stanley jumped at my side. He hissed, "Cassia, that bush over there moved! I saw it. Are the trees around here alive? Are we going to be eaten by an angry ash tree?"

I couldn't answer; I was too scared to. I watched the bush in front of us rustle in indignation. Then it moved. Legs appeared at its base and it lifted itself up and came slowly towards us, rustling menacingly as it did so. A strong smell of rotting leaves came with it.

Stanley nudged into my leg. "Magic! Use your magic!"

I raised my hand.

"There's no need for that!" a voice boomed out. It came from the bush. The leaves shook vigorously and then fell to the ground as one. A man stepped out from the leaves and bellowed, "What do you want? Can't you read? Didn't you see the sign on the door? Visitors are not welcome! Clear off!"

The man was hairy from head to toe. Thick, bushy eyebrows knitted together above his angry eyes. Long, straggly hair stuck to his large shoulders. His matted, dirty beard twitched in anger. He even had hair sprouting from his ears and nostrils.

I lifted my head and found a modicum of courage. "I'm Cassia Winter, and this is Stanley. We're looking for Mortimer." I stopped as I didn't know his last name. "Uncle to Nerita and Conway." I stopped again. I didn't know their last names either. Did merpeople even have surnames?

The man grunted. "What do you want with Mortimer?"

"That's for me to discuss with him. Do you know where I can find him?"

Stanley was sniffing the leaves. He looked up and said, "These aren't real; they're made of fabric. And that rotting smell is fake. Is this a costume? A disguise? It's a very good one."

The man suddenly laughed making me drop my broomstick in shock. I quickly retrieved it.

He knelt at Stanley's side, lifted the leafy material and said, "Yes, it's an excellent disguise. I made it myself. I'm an inventor. This is the perfect thing to wear when I'm going around this forest. I can spy on many a creature without them noticing me! I've made the material light and breathable. Would you like to try it on?"

"Yes, please," Stanley replied.

The man lifted a section of the costume carefully over Stanley.

From beneath his blanket of leaves, Stanley called out, "I'm a bush! A walking, talking bush! Look at me." He wriggled from side to side making the leaves rustle.

The man chuckled and removed the material from Stanley. "I've got some more disguises inside. You can have a look at them if you like? And you can try them on."

"Thank you!" Stanley began to move towards the cottage.

I held my hand up. "Whoa there, Stanley. You're not going anywhere with this strange man. We don't know who he is or what's inside his cottage."

The man straightened up, grabbed his hair and beard and pulled them right off. He ripped off his thick eyebrows and pulled at his nose and ear hairs until they were free. His eyes watered as he did so. "Too much glue," he explained.

Once the man was free of hair, I could see the family resemblance between him and King Taron.

"Mortimer?" I asked.

He nodded. "That's me. Sorry for all that rigmarole. I'm not the sociable type and when my radar spotted you flying this way, I decided to camouflage myself. The radar is another one of my inventions. You're a justice witch, aren't you? I don't go into town often, but I have heard your name mentioned recently. What are you doing here?"

"I wanted to talk to you about Nerita's suspicious death."

Mortimer blanched and staggered backwards. He put his hand towards a small boulder and lowered himself to it. "Pardon? Did you say death? Nerita is dead?"

I went over to his side. "Yes, she is. Sorry to be the bearer of bad news. I don't know why, but I assumed you'd know about her. Don't you keep in touch with any of the merpeople?"

He stared at the ground. "The only one I kept in touch with was Nerita. I saw her last week." He looked back at me. "When did she die? How? You mentioned a suspicious death. Do you mean murder? Is that why you're here?"

I seated myself on a smaller boulder at his side. "It is. I am sorry about Nerita. I've been making investigations and your name was mentioned. Nerita talked about you when she ordered the sirens to leave this world and go into another world. I think she sent them into the human world. What do you know about that?"

Mortimer ran his hand over his chin. "Not much. Nerita spoke to me last week about a threat somewhere in the seas. I asked her to clarify that, but she wouldn't. She said she was dealing with the matter on her own. She did mention the sirens were going to help her, but again, she wouldn't elaborate." His eyes were full of sadness as he continued, "We'd only become reunited a few years ago. She turned up here one day and demanded that I talk to her. She hadn't known about my existence until a drunken sea hag had told her everything about me and my terrible past. Despite knowing what I'd done, she came here and demanded an explanation. I had none. I had no excuse for what I did during my time as king of the merpeople. The power went to my head and I abused it. I've regretted it every day since. I explained this to her and said her father wouldn't be pleased that she was talking to me. But, being the stubborn kind, she refused to listen to me and continued to turn up here. I liked her company. She was …" His voice caught in his throat and he looked away.

"How did she come to visit you?" I asked. "I'm presuming she walked here or got a lift somehow. Wouldn't it have hurt her legs to travel so far from the sea?"

Mortimer nodded. "She used the flying unicorn taxis most of the time. But you're right about her legs hurting so far from the sea. She had a solution to that. She'd got a potion from that drunken sea hag to manage the pain during her visits here. I know it was selfish of me, but after a while, I encouraged her visits. I loved hearing about my old community. I've missed them so much and I certainly miss being in the sea." He let out a small laugh. "Call me foolish, but I was hoping that one day I could make things right between me and my brother. I was hoping Nerita could help me with that."

I waited a moment before saying, "Do you know if Nerita had any enemies?"

"She did mention another mermaid who she didn't get along with. Isla? Yes, I think that's the right name. Would you mind saving your questions for another time? I'd like to be alone for a while."

Without waiting for my answer, Mortimer stood up, went over to his leafy disguise and threw it over himself. He shuffled away into the dense forest.

Stanley and I watched him go. When he'd gone, Stanley said, "Shall I say it or are you going to say it?"

"That he's not telling us the whole truth? That he's keeping something from us? Is that what you're thinking?"

Stanley nodded. "Shall we go after him and ask him some more questions?"

"Not yet. I can see that he's genuinely upset. Let's leave him to grieve. We'll come back later." I stood up. "Let's go back to the apartment. I wonder if Jeremy has found anything else out about the merpeople yet?"

We headed straight back to the apartment. Jeremy wasn't there, but someone else was waiting for us. And that someone had collapsed on the pavement next to the apartment door.

Stanley hissed, "Is he dead?"

I quickly swooped down to the still figure. "I don't know."

Chapter 18

It was a white-faced Conway who was lying in a crumpled heap outside the apartment door with his eyes closed. His chest was heaving and his breathing laboured as he gasped for air.

We landed at his side and Stanley put his head on the merman's chest. He said, "He's struggling to breathe. I think he's going to die." He moved away and hopped from paw to paw in agitation. "Can you do something?"

"I'll try." I knelt at Conway's side and placed my hands inches above his chest. I kept my mind calm and pictured Conway breathing easily and looking normal again. The magical tingle came into my fingers and flowed into Conway's chest. The sound of his breathing was making me feel anxious, but I pushed that feeling away. My magic worked better when I was calm. I intensified the image in my mind of a healthy Conway. The tingle in my fingers grew and it felt more like pins and needles now.

Stanley put his head against Conway's chest again. "His breathing is becoming more regular. His heartbeat has returned to normal." He looked my way. "He's going to be alright. You saved him."

I sat back on my heels and wiggled my fingers to get rid of the sharp pain that lingered there.

Conway's eyes opened and focused on me. "Cassia? Is that you?"

I nodded.

Stanley put his paw on Conway's chin. "And it's me, Stanley. You nearly died! Cassia saved you."

Conway's eyes widened as he stared at me. "Did you? You saved my life?"

My cheeks suddenly felt warm. I flapped a hand dismissively at him. "It was nothing. Anyone would have done the same. Conway, what are you doing here? You're too far away from the sea. You must be in terrible pain." I reached out and pulled him into a sitting position. "How are you feeling?"

He winced. "Not good. I had to see you, Cassia. I had to see how far you'd got with the investigation. I – " He took a sharp intake of breath and pressed his lips together.

"You're still in pain," I said. "Let's get you into the café. Gilda might have something to help you. She has everything in that café." I held my hands out to help him up.

Conway's face twisted in pain. Through clenched teeth, he said, "I don't think I can move. My legs are hurting too much."

I immediately sent more magic into my fingers and moved them over Conway's legs. I concentrated on taking the pain away. There wasn't a tingle in my fingers this time; I experienced an intense pain which was like a hundred sewing needles were being jabbed into my hands. I clenched my teeth together to stop myself from crying out in agony.

Conway said, "It's working. Whatever you're doing is working. Thank you."

The stabbing feeling in my hands increased and I felt my eyes watering with pain. I couldn't stop now. I had to take all the pain from Conway. I'd never taken pain from someone before and I had no idea it was going to be so painful. I continued to focus on the work I was doing and did my best not to show I was in agony.

I felt a nudge at my side and saw Stanley's concerned face looking at me. In a quiet voice, he said, "Enough, Cassia, that's enough. You're hurting yourself."

I dropped my hands and rested them on my knees. They felt as if they'd been too near to a fire and I desperately wanted to run them under a cold tap.

Conway got to his feet and gingerly moved from side to side. "The pain has gone. All of it. Thank you, thank you so much."

I smiled up at Conway and attempted to get to my feet without using my sore hands. Stanley, bless him, put his paw out and tried to help me. I pressed my lips tightly together in effort as I slowly got to my feet.

After placing a bright smile on my face, I indicated my head towards the café door. and said, "Let's go inside."

Conway thankfully opened the door for us and stood to one side to let me through. My throbbing hands dangled uselessly at my side and I tried not to bump them into anything. Stanley came after me and walked closely by my side.

Gilda came over to us the second Conway closed the door behind him. Her eyes were wide with shock as she looked at Conway. "Conway! What are you doing here? You can't be this far from the sea!"

Conway smiled. "It's okay. Cassia has taken my pain away. She's marvellous."

Gilda's attention went to my hands and her eyes widened even more. "Cassia, you come with me immediately." She looked back at Conway. "You take a seat and I'll bring you some of Gia's bottled sea water. I keep some here for emergencies. Stanley, will you take Conway over to that corner table? Thank you."

"This way," Stanley said to Conway and he trotted over to the corner table.

Gilda put her hands on my shoulders and said, "Your hands! They look as if they've been burnt. Didn't you use a protective spell on yourself before taking Conway's pain away? That's what Blythe and your gran do."

I shrugged. "I panicked. I wasn't thinking straight." I looked down at my red hands. "I'll use magic on them. I'll heal myself."

"You can't heal yourself if your hands are damaged. Come with me."

Gilda took me to the back of the café and through the door that led to the kitchen. She guided me over to the sink and told me to hold my hands out over it. I did so and watched as she took a jug of clear liquid from the fridge. She waved one hand over it and muttered something. Was she casting a spell?

Gilda came to my side, lifted the jug and trickled the water gently over my injured hands.

The water was cold; icy cold. It felt wonderful as it dribbled over my hands and into the sink. Each drop of water alleviated the burning pain and I felt myself sighing with relief. Gilda continued pouring the water and I noticed the redness in my hands disappearing. By the time the jug was empty, my hands were back to their normal colour.

I lifted my hands and wiggled my fingers. "The pain has gone. All of it." I gave her a sideways look. "How did you do that? Are you a witch of some sort?"

Gilda smiled. "I have my secrets." Her smiled faded. "Cassia, don't ever perform that spell again without protecting yourself first. You could have damaged your hands forever. Okay?"

"Okay." I gave her a firm nod.

Gilda looked towards the door that led to the café. "What is that merman doing here anyway?"

"That's what I'm going to find out." I gave Gilda a grateful smile. "Thank you for helping me."

"I'm always here to help you. Go through to the café and I'll bring you something to eat and drink."

I said thank you again before leaving the kitchen. As soon as I walked into the café, I saw that Stanley and Conway had a visitor at their table. It was Luca. His face was red with anger and he was jabbing a finger in Conway's direction.

I quickly strode over to the table.

Luca turned his angry face my way and snapped, "What's this merman doing here? Is this your idea? Did you tell him to come here? Stanley said he'd collapsed outside your door. Don't you know what happens to merman when they're away from the sea? This is totally irresponsible of you."

Stanley said, "I tried to explain what happened to Conway and how you helped him, but Luca won't listen."

Conway added, "And I tried to tell him it was my idea to come here, and that you saved my life. But, like Stanley said, he won't listen."

"Of course I won't listen to your lies!" Luca exploded. "You're covering up for Cassia. She doesn't know what she's doing with this investigation." He turned on me. "That's the truth, isn't it? You don't know what you're doing. Explain yourself."

I looked into Luca's deep, blue eyes and remembered the friends we were. I knew he wasn't himself at the moment and getting into an argument with him wouldn't help matters at all.

I put my hand under Luca's elbow and pushed him towards the exit door. With my other hand, I opened the door wide. I was so glad my hands were feeling better or this dramatic gesture of mine wouldn't have been so effective.

In a firm voice, I said to Luca, "I know exactly what I'm doing and I don't need to explain myself to you. Get out."

Luca tried to wriggle free but my grip was vice-like. He spat, "You can't tell me what to do."

He looked like an angry toddler and I couldn't help but smile at him. Keeping a commanding tone in my voice, I continued, "Yes, I can tell you what to do. Get out. Now." I pushed him through the open door and onto the street. I gave him a friendly wave before shutting the door on his outraged face.

I returned to the table to see Conway and Stanley staring at me with admiration on their faces.

I took a seat and said, "Right, Conway, sorry about that. Tell me why you put your life in danger by coming to see me."

Chapter 19

Gilda came over at that point and put some plates and cups on the table. She handed a large cup to Conway and said, "Drink this water. It'll help you feel better. Cassia's spell and this water won't last long. You'll have to return to the sea soon."

"I will do," Conway took the cup. "Thank you."

Gilda gave me a concerned look before moving away. I looked at the plate she'd put in front of me. It contained a large slice of lemon drizzle cake. Yum. There was a cup of something green at the side which I picked up and sniffed. It was green tea with a hint of lemon. Knowing Gilda, the lemon in the cake and tea would make me feel better emotionally and physically in no time.

I lowered a section of the table in front of Stanley so that he could reach the bowl Gilda had put there for him. He smacked his lips together and said, "I think it's cream. Gilda has the best cream here. It makes me feel warm and fuzzy inside. It's like a hug in a bowl." He gave his full attention to the bowl and smiled lovingly at it.

Conway drained his cup and placed it on the table. "Cassia, I'm sorry for putting you to so much trouble. I wasn't thinking straight when I set off this morning. I did get a flying unicorn taxi for most of the way here and thought I'd be fine. But I've been waiting outside your door for a while and that's when the pain kicked in. I'm terribly sorry. I'm such a nuisance."

"You're not a nuisance at all. Tell me why you wanted to see me." I scooped some of the cake into my mouth. It was soft and zingy. A cool feeling travelled down my body and settled in my hands. It was like getting into a refreshingly cold shower at the end of a warm and sticky day.

Conway continued, "It's Father. He's in a terrible state. He hasn't slept since Nerita died. He's convinced that someone in another community killed her. He thinks she gathered the sirens to form a secret army, and one of the other leaders found out about it and decided to stop her before she went to war."

I frowned. "That doesn't make sense. Would she really go to war with another community without telling your father or you? And would she form a secret army?"

"I don't know. Nerita liked to be in control, and she liked to keep problems to herself. She could have received threats from the other leaders and decided to sort matters out herself. Father is convinced we are going to be attacked any day as a result of Nerita forming an army."

"Has anyone heard from the sirens yet?" I asked.

"No. I believe Rex is still looking for them."

I raised my cake fork at him. "Ah. Speaking of Rex, did you know he was in a relationship with your sister?"

"Rex and Nerita? Are you sure about that?"

I nodded. "Isla told me."

Conway smiled down at the table. "If Isla told you, then it must be true. Isla finds out everything." He looked back at me. "She's going to make a wonderful leader one day. I know people think she's bossy, but she gets things done."

I considered whether or not I should mention Isla's previous engagements. But I was dealing with a murder investigation and despite her fiancé sitting in front of me, Isla was a suspect.

I said to Conway, "Do you know about Isla's previous engagements to other mermen?"

Conway nodded. "Oh yes, we are very truthful with each other. She told me about the prince she was engaged to before she met me. She had to break it off with him because he was too clingy."

Stanley looked up from his bowl. "One prince? She was engaged to just one prince?"

Conway gave him a wary look. "Yes, that's what she told me. Do you know something different?"

I shifted in my seat. "Well, yes. We were told Isla's been engaged more than once."

Conway's face fell. "Has she? I didn't know that. Perhaps I should have a word with Isla when I return home."

I pushed my empty cake plate to one side. "I hope I haven't caused you any trouble by telling you that."

"Of course not. I'm glad you told me." Conway placed his hands on the table and said, "How far have you got with your investigation? Do you know who killed my sister yet? I'd like to give Father some positive news."

"I'm still making enquiries. Do you know you have an Uncle Mortimer?"

Conway blanched. "Yes, I do know about him. I remember him from a long time ago. Father never talks about him, but I know what Mortimer did when he was king. Why are you asking about him? Has he got something to do with Nerita's death?"

"I'm not sure yet. We spoke to him a short while ago. Nerita had been visiting him for the past few years."

Conway shook his head rapidly. "This isn't good news at all. Mortimer must be up to something. He must have been making plans to take the crown from Father. From what I've heard about him, he's a nasty creature and only cares for himself." He continued shaking his head. "This isn't good news at all! I have to tell Father immediately." He became still and gave me an intense look. "Do you think Mortimer killed Nerita? If he wanted to take the crown from Father, he might have wanted her out of the way first."

"I don't know. I'm sorry." I felt helpless and realised I should have asked Mortimer more questions while I had the chance. "I'll speak to him again very soon."

Conway nodded. "Thank you." He glanced out of the window. "I think it's time I went home. I'll order a unicorn taxi." He flinched and his nostrils flared.

"Are you in pain again?" I asked.

He gave me a tight smile. "The pain is coming back a little."

I stood up. "I'll take you back to the beach on my broomstick. It'll be a bit of squeeze on there with all of us, but it'll be quicker." I held my hand up. "I don't want any arguments. Come on."

We left the café and got on my broomstick. Conway sat behind me and held onto my waist too tightly. There was a tremor in his voice as he said, "This broomstick is quite narrow, isn't it? Have you ever fallen off?"

"Not yet," I replied. "Hold on tight!"

We rose into the sky and I cast a silent spell on the broomstick to make it fly faster. It worked immediately and we shot forwards at a speed which took my breath away. My adrenalin junkie of a cat loved it and whooped with delight as we raced through the air.

We covered the ten miles to the beach in less than five minutes. The lemon drizzle cake in my stomach was not happy about that and threatened to make a reappearance. As soon as we landed, I put a hand on my whirling stomach and sent a quick shot of healing to it.

Conway collapsed to the sand in front of me and put a hand on his sweaty forehead. He mumbled, "So fast. We went so fast." He moved his hand and said to me, "Thank you for getting me here so quickly. I didn't know you could go so fast. You are an amazing witch, Cassia Winter."

Stanley was dancing about on the sand and yelling, "Awesome! That was awesome! Let's do it again! Yeah!"

I shook my head at him and then helped Conway to his feet. He grimaced and said, "Can you help me into the sea, please?"

I put my arms around him and guided him towards the water. He leant heavily on me and I tried not to collapse under his weight. Stanley declared he would stay on the sand and watch us.

Conway's face was scrunched up with effort as we continued along the sand.

"Just a few more steps," I told him.

I was huffing and puffing as I helped him walk towards the sea. He was still leaning on me for support and I was sure I was going to collapse at any second. We reached the water and waded in. I felt Conway taking some of his weight off me.

When we were in deep enough, Conway ducked into the water and swam out a little. His legs were immediately replaced by a tail and he flapped it happily in the water. He turned onto his back, looked at me and gave me a big smile. "We made it! Thank you! Thank you so much!"

He suddenly stopped smiling and looked over his shoulder to the sea behind him. He turned back to me and yelled, "Cassia! There's a siren behind me! She's in distress. Come here quickly!"

Chapter 20

I looked back at Stanley and made a gesture to show him I was going into the sea. He gave me a nod but stayed where he was.

I pulled off my shoes and socks and flung them to one side. Conway had swum up to the water's edge and was holding his hand to me, his tail flapping gently behind him. I waded into the water and grabbed Conway's hand.

He said, "It's time to show you how fast I can move now. Take a deep breath."

I did so and Conway tugged on my hand as we shot through the water. My poor stomach heaved in protest. I was going to end up with a bad case of digestion at this rate.

Conway pulled me along the surface of the water at an incredible speed and by the time I let out my breath, we were near a creature bobbing in the water.

Conway nodded towards her and said to me, "This is Syloe. She's one of the youngest sirens." He smiled at Syloe. "Hello. What are you doing out here on your own? Where's your family?"

The pale creature with long hair moved her head sadly from side to side. She moaned, "They've gone. I lost them. I can't find them. Have you seen them? Where are they?" She let out a long, low moan which made my ears throb with pain.

Conway moved closer to Syloe. "Where have you been? You've been missing for days. Are you hurt?"

Syloe whined, "My heart hurts. My poor heart. Where is my family? They were right in front of me, and now they're gone. Oooooooo!"

Her soulful cries were now making my ears vibrate. They'd never vibrated before and it wasn't a pleasant experience. I decided to take over the questioning.

"Syloe, hi, I'm Cassia. Did Nerita ask you and the other sirens to go into another world?"

The sad siren nodded. "Yes. I didn't like it. It was noisy. There was a strange bird in the sky. It roared and it was shiny. I think it must have been a dragon bird because smoke came from its tail."

Was she talking about an aeroplane?

I continued, "Do you know the name of the world you went into?"

Syloe shook her head and swished her hands from side to side in the water. "I'm all alone now. All alone."

I persisted, "Why did you go into that other world? What did Nerita tell you?"

Syloe stopped moving her hands and put her head to one side. "The seabed. Yes, that's what she said. The seabed has been damaged by that black cloud and something terrible was going to happen in that world. Uncle Mortimer knows! That's what Nerita said. Uncle Mortimer knows about the seabed and that black cloud. Nerita sent us to that noisy world so we could collect the people when the terrible thing happens."

"What terrible thing?" I asked.

Syloe put her hands to the side of her face and wailed, "I don't know! But it's going to be so terrible. Awful. A catastrophe! Nerita knows. Uncle Mortimer knows. Where is my family? Where did they go?" She let out a long wail which made my left ear pop painfully.

I moved closer to Syloe and placed a hand on her cold shoulder in an attempt to calm her down. "What happened to your family? When did you last see them?"

Syloe moved her hands. "I don't know. I went with them to that other world. We were waiting for the terrible thing to happen. Then I saw that awful, noisy bird in the sky. It scared me! I swam away from it. But it was faster than me. It kept following me. I went under the sea and kept swimming until I felt safe." She looked around her. "And I came here. I feel safe here. But where is my family?"

"I don't know," I told her. "But I'll do my best to find them." I moved away from her and said quietly to Conway, "I don't know what to make of that. From what I can gather, Nerita told the sirens to go into my world for some reason. I think it has something to do with the black magic that came into this area recently. I need to find Mortimer and speak to him about it. I'd still like to speak to Rex too."

Conway nodded. "I'll look out for Rex. I'll speak to Father about Mortimer too in case he knows what he's been up to lately." He looked towards Syloe who was now singing a sorrowful song. "I'll look after Syloe. Do you want help getting back to the beach?"

"No, thank you. It's not that far away." I looked back at Syloe and my heart twisted at the grief on her face. "I need to find those missing sirens as soon as possible. If something terrible is going to happen in my world, I want to know about it."

Conway gave me a short smile before moving over to Syloe.

I swam back to the beach and quickly dried myself using my magic hands. I held my socks and shoes in my hands as I walked back to Stanley. I appreciated the feeling of warm sand between my toes. If I wasn't dealing with a murder enquiry, I would have loved to have taken the rest of the day off to lounge on this beautiful beach.

As I got closer to Stanley, I noticed something different about him.

He raised a paw to his nose and said, "Look, I've got a friend."

A pale, green butterfly was resting on his nose. When I came closer, it alighted and headed in my direction. I opened my hand out and it landed on my palm. It opened its wings and Oliver's voice boomed out:

'Cassia, Stanley, you need to come home immediately!" His voice became quieter as he continued, 'Cassia, I've found something that belongs to your mum. I think it's

going to help you with your investigation. See you soon.
Oliver.'

Chapter 21

We found Oliver sitting on a chair next to the kitchen table in Gran's house. There was a small, shell-covered box on the table in front of him.

Without any welcoming words, Oliver waved his paw at the box and said to me, "Open that."

Stanley jumped up onto the chair next to Oliver and said, "Hello brother. Are you okay?"

Oliver replied, "Yes, I'm fine." He looked Stanley over and said, "You look tired. Hasn't Cassia given you any time to rest or have a nap? Has she been feeding you?"

Stanley chuckled and gave him a nod. "There's no need to worry; Cassia takes good care of me."

I moved over to the box and stared down at it. I'd seen this box before somewhere. The small shells that decorated it had tiny flecks of silver and gold glitter in them and they caught the sun's rays which were coming through the kitchen window. I had a feeling that I knew who this box belonged to.

Oliver said briskly, "Don't stand there looking daft; open the box." He gave me a studied look and his tone softened, "It belonged to your mum."

I gave him a nod and tried to speak. My voice was gruff as I said, "I know, it used to be in Mum's bedroom. I haven't seen it for years. Where did you find it?"

Oliver looked to one side and shrugged his little shoulders. There was a hint of embarrassment in his voice as he explained, "I was doing some dusting before Esther came back and I came across it in the very back of her wardrobe."

I folded my arms and gave him a smile. "Oh? Does it get very dusty at the back of Gran's wardrobe?"

Oliver didn't meet my glance as he continued, "I've seen Esther putting things in there before, but she always told me they were personal items and that I shouldn't stick my nose in there. But with her being away, I thought there might be some clues as to where she's gone in there." He looked back at me and defended himself, "It's a good job I did investigate because that's where I found that box. I recognised it immediately. Well? Aren't you going to open it?"

I asked him, "Haven't you already opened it?"

"Of course I have. I wouldn't have called you here if there wasn't something important inside."

Without any further ado, I opened the small box and looked inside. There was a key in there. I picked it up and showed it to Stanley. It was a long, old-fashioned kind of key made out of brass. The top of the key had been moulded into the shape of a butterfly and two tiny gems had been placed at the top of the butterfly's wings.

Stanley examined the key and said, "That's a beautiful key. What does it unlock? A treasure chest? A secret stash of chocolate in a hidden room? A hidden passageway to somewhere amazing?"

Oliver moved his mouth in what looked suspiciously like a smile and said, "Even better than that. It unlocks the door to the lighthouse in Brimstone Beach."

My eyebrows shot up in surprise. "The lighthouse? In Brimstone Beach?"

Oliver said, "That's right; that's what I said. Have you gone deaf?"

Stanley's voice was full of excitement as he proclaimed, "We saw that lighthouse! We flew near it yesterday. It's painted in the colours of the Brimstone butterflies. Why does Cassia's mum have a key to it?"

"Because she owned it," Oliver explained. He gave me a kind look and continued, "And now, it belongs to you, Cassia. I'm sure your Gran would have told you about it one day."

I turned the key over in my hand. "There are a lot of things that Gran is planning to tell me one day. When she comes back, I'll be having a long conversation with her." I looked back at Oliver. "Thank you for finding this. You said in your message that it might help us with our investigation. What did you mean by that?"

Oliver said, "Your mum spent a lot of time with the merpeople and other creatures at the beach. I know she kept records of her dealings with them. I've had a good search of Esther's house, and I can't find any of Rosalyn's records here. She did spend time at the lighthouse and I suspect her records may be somewhere inside. I think it would be worth going to the lighthouse for a visit, don't you?"

Stanley leapt off the chair and said, "Let's go right now. I've never been in a lighthouse before. Can we see if the light works at the top of it? Can I switch it on and off?"

I gave him a small nod before saying to Oliver, "I've got a strange feeling that I've been to the lighthouse before. Is that possible?"

Oliver surprised me by jumping onto the kitchen table and moving over to me. He rested a paw on my arm and said, "I think you used to go there with your mum when you were younger. She did take you to Brimstone Beach many times and I'm sure she would have taken you to the lighthouse too. Will you be alright going there? I could come with you. I know this is a difficult time for you with Esther and Blythe being gone and all this new information about your mum coming to the surface. Not to mention that you've got that murder investigation to deal with."

I smiled at him and said, "Actually, I think this is the perfect time for me to find out more about Mum. Instead of feeling upset, all this new information is making me happy and I can feel Mum's presence around me."

Oliver patted my arm and removed his paw. "That's good. Before you dash off to the lighthouse, do you want to tell me what's been going on with your investigation? Are you any closer to finding out who killed that poor mermaid?"

I pulled a chair out and sat down. I kept the key in my hand as it felt comforting there. Stanley jumped onto my knee and settled himself. Between us, we told Oliver about our investigation so far and ended with what Syloe had told us about going into the human world.

I said to Oliver, "How would the sirens get into our world? Are there some doorways somewhere or any underwater passageways?"

"It's possible," Oliver replied. "It wouldn't surprise me if someone had used black magic to make their way into our world. Didn't you say a black cloud had been hovering over the sea a while back? You could ask Jeremy about that, and if he knows about any secret passageways. Speaking of Jeremy, where is he?"

"That's a good question," I said. "I think he's still making investigations about this case. I'll catch up with him soon. Oliver, what do you think about the investigation so far?"

Oliver settled himself down on the table. "There are a number of suspects that come to mind, the first one being Isla. It could be a simple case of her being jealous about Nerita being in charge of Brimstone Beach and maybe Isla wanted her out of the way before she gets married to Conway. If she is as power-mad as you've heard, then getting rid of Nerita would make sense." Oliver raised his paw to make his next point. "Then there's Rex to consider. It's interesting that he never mentioned his relationship with Nerita. I wonder how long they'd been a couple? And why they broke up? That's another line of enquiry for you to consider. Once you find Rex, that is."

I gave him a knowing look. "Supernatural creatures in Brimstone have a habit of disappearing just when I need to interrogate them. What do you think about this business with Nerita's uncle? He was keeping something from me. I think he knows where the sirens have gone."

"The missing sirens could be nothing to do with Nerita's death, but it's worth making further enquiries with her uncle." Oliver put his head to one side and gave me a long look. "Cassia, don't take this the wrong way, but you have to stop being so feeble when you question your suspects. Try to get the truth out of them immediately and don't take any nonsense from them. Have you thought about doing any assertiveness courses? There are some online ones that you can take. I can give you the links." He let out a gruff chuckle. "I've managed to become quite proficient at using my paws on the computer. I've even got my own Facebook account."

Stanley came to my defence. "Oliver, Cassia acts in a professional manner when she questions suspects. But there are some sneaky beings out there, and they often keep the truth from us. But Cassia and I always get to the bottom of the truth - eventually." He paused a fraction. "Can you set up a Facebook account for me too? Are there other cats on Facebook?"

I said, "Can we leave talk about your online social activities for another time, please? I want to go over to the lighthouse now and see if there's anything there that might help us. Oliver, I appreciate your opinion and I'll try to be more aggressive with my questions. You can come with us. It would be nice to have your company."

"No, thanks. I'm going to carry on with my cleaning work here. I know that Esther will be returning very soon." He gave me a sharp nod. "She'll be back very soon. I can feel it in my whiskers."

We stayed with Oliver for a few more minutes to make sure he was okay being on his own, and then we said goodbye to him. He told us to keep in touch and reminded me to be more aggressive with my suspects and to stop being such a namby-pamby excuse of a witch. I knew his abrupt words concealed his concern, so I wasn't insulted. Not too much.

Stanley and I gave him a last wave before going through the cellar door to Brimstone. I put the lighthouse key safely in my pocket, jumped onto my broomstick with Stanley and soared into the sky.

What was I going to find inside Mum's lighthouse?

Chapter 22

We landed in front of the pale, yellow wooden door set at the bottom of the lighthouse. There were low bushes to either side of the door and I smiled at the dozen or so Brimstone butterflies who were resting on the leaves.

The second we touched the ground, Stanley leapt off the broomstick and began to run around the building.

When he came back to my side he announced, "It's round! It's round all the way around. There's not one corner anywhere! Isn't it amazing? I think I'll go around it again." He scampered off before I could say a word.

I gazed at the yellow door and felt a warmth settle over me as if someone had just wrapped me in a blanket. Even though my memories weren't clear, I knew for certain that I had been here before.

I waited for Stanley to finish his latest inspection of the lighthouse before inserting the key into the lock. Before I could turn it, someone landed at my side and declared, "There you are! I've been looking for you two all over the place."

I smiled at Jeremy and said, "We were hoping to catch up with you. Where have you been?"

Jeremy placed his broomstick on the ground. "I've been talking to everyone I possibly can about Nerita and the other merpeople. I can now conclude that I have no new information for you. Everyone says Nerita was bossy, but effective in her work, and that Isla was jealous of her. I've tried to dig up some gossip in the town centre, but it appears the majority of the creatures who live there don't know much about the merpeople. So, in essence, it's been a complete waste of time." He sighed heavily.

"It wasn't a complete waste of time as you've confirmed what we already knew." I pointed to the key which was sticking out of the lock. "Look what Oliver found. I didn't even know this lighthouse belonged to Mum."

Jeremy's cheeks flushed red. "You didn't? Didn't I tell you? I could have sworn I told you on our first visit here." He put his hands over his face and let out a low groan. "What an idiot I am!" He removed his hands. "I'm so sorry for not telling you. I used to come here all the time with Rosalyn. Why didn't I tell you?" He shook his head in disbelief.

"You've had a lot on your mind, Jeremy," I reassured him. "You probably did tell me, but I wasn't listening properly. It doesn't matter now. Oliver said Mum might have kept records of her dealings with the merpeople. Do you know if she did?"

Jeremy nodded. "Yes, I think she's got some notebooks somewhere inside." A small smile tugged at his mouth. "I think you'll like what's inside. I put a spell on the inside of the lighthouse when Rosalyn passed over to make sure dust never settled on anything. Everything should be just as she left it. Are you sure you're ok to go inside? I know you came here with Rosalyn and the memories may come back to you." His eyes glistened. "They're going to come back for me too."

I gave him a reassuring smile. "I'm excited. I can't wait to see inside." I turned the key in the lock and heard a loud click.

Something peculiar happened. The butterflies on the bushes at our side rose and moved behind me. There was a disturbance in the air and I felt my hair gently moving back from my face. The noise of many fluttering wings sounded out.

Stanley turned around and his eyes widened in shock. He raised a shaking paw at something in front of him. I spun around to see what he was looking at. Jeremy did the same and let out a half-strangled gasp.

We watched in amazement as hundreds of yellow and green Brimstone butterflies headed our way. Their fluttering wings sent a warm breeze over me and a feeling of excitement ignited in my stomach.

The cloud of butterflies hovered a few feet in front of us and moved closer to each other.

At my feet, Stanley whispered, "What are they doing? Are they making some sort of shape? Are they trying to tell us something?"

The butterflies settled themselves into a more recognisable shape.

Jeremy's voice trembled as he said, "This can't be happening. I can't believe what my eyes are seeing."

I smiled as the butterflies formed a large 3D image of Mum's head and shoulders. The butterflies stopped moving their wings and Mum's features became clearer.

Stanley leant his shaking body against my legs and whimpered, "Cassia, I don't like it. It's scary."

I picked him up. "It isn't scary at all. I think it's a message from Mum. Stanley, look at Mum's lovely face. The butterflies have got her features just right. They're even making her eyes blink."

Jeremy said, "You must have triggered the butterflies when you opened the lock. How did Rosalyn know you'd be coming here?"

Mum's butterfly lips opened and her lovely voice came out, "Cassia, my beautiful daughter, if you're receiving this message it means that I'm not there at your side and I apologise for that. Our work as justice witches is dangerous and I always knew there was a risk that I wouldn't see you grow into the beautiful young woman that I'm sure you now are."

A small butterfly rolled down Mum's cheek and looked like a tear falling.

Jeremy was sobbing quietly, but I didn't feel anywhere close to tears. A wonderful warm feeling was flowing through my body like the gentle warmth of the sun. Seeing Mum's face in butterfly form was making me feel incredibly loved. I basked in the feeling.

Mum continued, "I'm glad you found your way to this lighthouse. If you are here as part of your investigation work, you will find many of my notebooks tucked away inside." Her lips moved into a smile. "You will also find many other delightful things that I've kept for you over the years including letters I've written to you in case I wasn't going to be around." Her lips wobbled and another butterfly rolled down her cheek.

Jeremy broke into louder sobs and slid to the ground with his head in his hands. I knew I should comfort him but I wanted to hear what else Mum had to say so I ignored him for the moment.

Mum continued, "I thought this way of delivering a message would be a good idea, but now that I'm saying the words, I can see how difficult this is for me. I hope it's not too hard for you to receive this message." She attempted another smile which only caused more butterflies to act as tears. "Maybe I won't need to send this message. Maybe I'll be right at your side when you begin your work as a justice witch. Maybe."

My heart twisted at the pain in her face. The butterflies were doing a remarkable job of catching her every emotion.

Mum cleared her throat and said, "Cassia, I'm going to stop this message now because I feel like I'm going to burst into tears soon and I don't want the poor butterflies to replicate that. I'm glad you've made your way to this amazing part of Brimstone and I know you'll enjoy discovering my belongings, and yours, inside the lighthouse. You have been a blessing in my life and I love you so very much. Remember that always. I love you so very much."

Her last few words were barely audible and many butterflies tears tumbled down her cheeks. Jeremy was becoming hysterical with his cries now and Stanley let out little sobs in my arms.

I watched as the butterflies slowly dispersed until Mum's face was no longer visible. But the butterflies hadn't finished with me yet. They rearranged themselves into the shape of two big arms and moved towards me. They enveloped me in those arms and an intense feeling of love swept through me. I'd never felt anything like it before and it was incredibly powerful. I felt more alive than I had done for years.

All too soon, the Mum/butterfly hug was over. The butterflies flapped their wings gently at me before fluttering away.

Stanley raised his little head and said, "That was beautiful."

"It was," I agreed. I looked down at Jeremy. "There's no need for tears. Mum wouldn't want us to be sad."

Jeremy turned his blotchy, red face to me, sniffed and said, "I know. I can't help it. I'm such a wimp. You should send me back to my hometown immediately. I've been no use to you, no use at all."

I put Stanley down then pulled Jeremy to his feet. I wiped his tears away and said, "We'll have none of that, Mr Spring. I have loved having you with me and you've been very helpful. Let's go inside now. There could be important information waiting for us." I gave him a bright smile.

He puffed his chest out. "Right, I'm ready. I'll try to keep myself together."

I turned back to the lighthouse door and pushed it open.

Chapter 23

We stepped through the door and onto a welcome mat which had been decorated with many varieties of butterflies, not just the Brimstone ones. I inhaled and immediately detected the light aroma of Mum's perfume. It immediately took me back to my childhood days and I remembered how she used to put a little squirt of her rose perfume behind my ears.

Stanley was already scampering up the spiral stairs to our left so I followed him. I noticed the images of many sea creatures painted on the wall as I ascended. Behind me, Jeremy intermittently let out a small sob which was quickly followed by an apology.

He said, "It's just as I remember. Every little detail. Oh, the good times I had here with Rosalyn! The memories are flooding back."

We found Stanley at the top of the stairs staring out into the circular room. He shook his head slowly and said, "It's a round room. There's not one single corner; not one."

I leant down and stroked his head. "What did you think it was going to be like inside?"

Stanley looked up at me and replied, "You never know in this town." He turned his attention back to the room. "Isn't it beautiful in here? I love all the pastel colours and paintings on the walls. The furniture looks the same as what Esther has in her house. And it smells so fresh, almost like roses."

"That'll be Mum's perfume," I said to him. "You can't stand there forever; go and investigate."

Stanley nodded and padded further into the room.

I took a moment to look around. The room had a living area to one side complete with a large, comfy-looking sofa, and a small kitchen to the other. There was a curtained-off area opposite the living area, and through a gap in the curtains, I could see a double bed. There were two bookcases near the sofa which were packed with DVDs. I smiled as I recognised the mystery shows that Mum and I watched together. Being so young, I never understood what was going on, but Mum always tried to explain them to me.

Jeremy pointed to the TV at the side of the bookcases and said, "I thought that was an enchanted box until your mum explained it was a television set. She said they're very common in your world. This is where we used to watch things on the box together." He nodded in the direction of the curtained-off area. "There are some drawers under the bed and I think that's where Rosalyn kept her notebooks."

"I'll have a look at those soon," I told him. I stepped further into the room and walked over to one of the windows. It looked out over Brimstone Beach to the right and I could see a few merpeople sitting on the sand talking amongst themselves.

Stanley trotted over to my side and said, "There's a fridge over there. Do you think there will be any food inside? All this exploring has made me hungry."

"I doubt there will be anything inside it," I said, "unless…" I walked over to the fridge and opened it. "unless," I continued, "the lovely Gia has put some food in here for us. Which she has."

I picked up the note which was resting against a plate of sandwiches and read it:

'Cassia, I had the strongest feeling that you would be visiting your mum's lighthouse soon so I thought I'd pop a few things in the fridge for you and Stanley. I hope this is ok with you. Love, Gia.'

Stanley let out a little chuckle. "She's just like her sister. They are so thoughtful. What has she put in there for me?" He poked his nose into the fridge.

I gave him a few seconds to have a good sniff and I looked at the painting on the wall behind the fridge. More merpeople. The images showed mermaids and merman swimming hand in hand. The mermaids had sparkling

125

combs in their hair. There was a large painting of a wedding ceremony too. Everyone looked extremely happy.

Jeremy noticed me looking at the pictures and said, "It's been a long time since we had a wedding at Brimstone Beach. I hope Conway is able to go ahead with his marriage to Isla despite the loss of his sister."

Stanley turned his head away from the fridge and said, "Unless Isla is the one who murdered his sister. Then she won't be going anywhere. Cassia, there's a tub of cream at the back of the fridge. Would you mind pouring some for me, please?"

Jeremy said, "Let me do that for you, my friend. I need to make myself useful." He looked at me and suggested, "Why don't you have a look at the bedroom area and see if you can find those notebooks?"

"That's a good idea."

I walked over to the curtained-off area and pulled one of the curtains back. My heart gave a little leap of joy as I noticed the two pillows on the bed. One of them had Mum's name embroidered on it, and the other one had mine. A flash of a memory came to me and I recalled how I used to lie in this bed with Mum after a day at the beach. I could almost feel her hand brushing my hair to one side. I remember lying on the bed, looking up and seeing stars. Stars? Was that right?

I lowered myself onto the bed and looked upwards. Tiny, twinkling stars had been painted on the ceiling. I recalled how Mum had asked me to count them before falling asleep. Of course, I never managed to count them all. And, being young, I couldn't count to high numbers anyway.

I settled myself more comfortably on the bed and gazed up at the stars. My eyes felt heavy and I decided to close them just for a moment.

The next thing I knew, Stanley was whispering in my ear and telling me to wake up. I woke up with a start and looked around me. It took me a second to remember where I was. The room was dark now and lamps had been lit around it.

I sat up abruptly and said, "What happened? How long have I been asleep? What day is it?"

Stanley explained, "It's still the same day. You fell asleep for a few hours. You looked so peaceful lying there that Jeremy and I decided to let you have a rest. Did you have a good sleep?"

"I had a wonderful sleep. I was dreaming about being at the beach with Mum. We made the most enormous sandcastle. Have you had something to eat and drink?"

"Yes, Jeremy sorted me out. He found your mum's notebooks and he's taken them back to The Brimstone Hotel. He said he wants to go through them carefully and that you should have the night off and just enjoy being here. I agree with him."

"That's kind of Jeremy to do that for me. I hope he finds something useful."

Stanley said, "He also found some letters that your mum has written to you. He's put them on the bedside table."

I turned my head and looked at the pile of letters which had been tied up with a pink ribbon.

Stanley continued, "There are thirty letters. Are you going to read them now?"

I shook my head. "I'll wait until this investigation is over." I smiled at the letters. "I can't wait to read them, but if I start now I know that all thoughts of the investigation will go out of my mind."

"You've got more self-control than I have," Stanley said. "There are some sandwiches in the fridge for you. I think you should have something to eat."

"Maybe later. I'm not very hungry yet." Shall we continue investigating the lighthouse? The light at the top must be on by now. I want to see how it works. Do you want to come with me or are you ready to settle down for the night?"

Stanley had already leapt off the bed before I'd finished my sentence. "Let's go!" he declared and jogged towards the second set of stairs at the left of the room.

Stanley raced up the stairs and I ran after him. We came to a door at the top and Stanley stood to one side to allow me to open it. We walked out onto a small, circular area which had a round, glass room in the middle of it. Light was pouring from the room. A balcony ran around the glass room and there was a chest-high wooden rail on the outer edge of the balcony. I moved over to the glass room and peeped inside. A tiny piece of stone had been placed on a table in the middle of the room and a glass dome was protecting it. I picked Stanley up so that he could see it.

Stanley said, "That looks like shadowstone. Wow. That tiny piece is giving off all this light."

We'd come across shadowstone before. It was a magical substance which provided heat and electricity to Brimstone.

Keeping Stanley in my arms, I walked away from the glass room and had a stroll around the balcony. We could see the moonlight reflecting off the sea and heard the water rolling along the sand. At the other side of the balcony, I could just make out the distant lights of Brimstone town. It seemed very far away.

We listened to the gentle crashing of the waves for a few minutes and then returned to the main room. Stanley insisted that I have something to eat before going to bed. I did so and thoroughly enjoyed the cheese and pesto sandwich that Gia had made for me.

It wasn't long before the emotions of the day began taking their toll on me. I settled into the bed with Stanley at my side. We snuggled down into the covers and said goodnight to each other. With the sound of the waves in the distance and Stanley snoring gently at my side, I was soon fast asleep.

When I opened my eyes in the morning, my feelings of peace fled in a second. On the floor in front of me was a sparkling hair comb. It looked like Isla's hair comb.

Chapter 24

As soon as Stanley woke up, I showed him the comb.

"Is it the same one?" he asked. "Does it belong to Isla?"

"I think so. I've had a good look at it and it seems to be identical. Stanley, I don't like the idea of Isla coming into the lighthouse when we're asleep."

"If it was her," Stanley pointed out. "She denied putting it in Esther's apartment and she told us someone stole it from her. What if the same creature stole it from her again and placed it here? Perhaps they're trying to give us a strong message about Isla?"

"You could be right." I stroked his little head. "Did you have a good sleep?"

Stanley stretched out across the bedcover. "I had a marvellous sleep and I'm ready for a day of action."

"I'm ready to get aggressive with my interrogations. I'm determined to track Rex down and find out exactly what went on with him and Nerita." I stood up and moved over to the kitchen area. "After breakfast, of course."

"Of course," Stanley agreed.

It was another thirty minutes before we were ready to leave the beautiful lighthouse.

Before we left, Stanley said, What about your mum's letters? Are you going to take them with you?"

I shook my head. "I'll come back for them later. It will be something to look forward to."

We left the circular room and heading down the stairs. The door at the bottom was ajar and the key was on the inside of the lock.

Stanley sniffed the bottom of the door and declared, "It smells like the sea." His nose wrinkled in disgust.

I examined the door and said, "Everything smells like the sea around here. There's no sign of forced entry to the lock. I wonder if Jeremy locked the door when he left last night?"

"He can't have done," Stanley pointed out, "if the key is on the inside of the door. Unless he used magic to secure it when he left? He might have done that."

We left the lighthouse and I made sure the door was securely locked before turning away from it. A yellow butterfly fluttered over to me and hovered in the air. I held my hand out and it landed on my palm. Jeremy's voice sounded urgent as he declared:

'Cassia, come quickly to the café! I'm holding Rex prisoner. You need to get here as quickly as you can because I'm not sure how long I can keep him here. He's a big chap. Love from Jeremy.'

I gave the butterfly a reply to say we were on our way. We jumped onto my broomstick and headed towards the café. Despite being little, the butterfly was ahead of us all the way.

When we walked into the café, we noticed Gia standing near the counter with her arms folded and a grim expression on her face.

I walked over to her and said, "Thank you for filling the fridge up in the lighthouse. We really appreciate it."

She gave me a small nod. "You are more than welcome. I hope you're here to talk to Rex. Jeremy is struggling to keep him tied up." She pointed towards the corner of the café and continued, "Rex is going to be out of those magical ropes any second now."

I looked towards the corner of the café and saw Rex pinned to a chair by an invisible force. His face was red with effort as he attempted to move his arms and legs. Jeremy was standing a short distance away with his arms outstretched and flashes of green light were shooting from his fingers. Jeremy's face was just as red as Rex's.

I quickly walked over to them and said to Jeremy, "What's going on? What are you doing to him?"

Jeremy wheezed, "I've used invisible ropes to bind him to that chair. But I can't hold my magic in place much longer. Have you seen the size of his muscles? Can you do something to help me?"

Rex called out, "Release me! Immediately! I've done nothing wrong to warrant this kind of imprisonment. I only came in here for a bottle of water."

I said to Jeremy, "Thank you for holding him here. You can stop using your magic now. I'm sure we can be civilised about this." I turned my attention to Rex and said, "I'd like to ask you a few questions about Nerita."

"I have told you all that you need to know about Nerita. Tell your colleague to release me immediately. I won't say another word until he does." He clamped his mouth shut to emphasise his point.

I looked at Jeremy who still had his hands raised towards Rex. "Jeremy, release him before you burst with the effort of holding him in place."

Letting out a loud sigh of relief, Jeremy dropped his hands and collapsed into the nearest chair. I heard a scrape of chair legs at my side and saw Rex leaping to his feet. He raised his fist in Jeremy's direction and snarled, "You'll pay for this! Stand up so I can knock you down!"

As Rex advanced on the quivering Jeremy, I declared, "That's enough! There won't be any fighting in here; that's an order."

Rex's fist hovered in the air and he looked uncertain as to what he should do.

I repeated, "That's an order. Rex, sit down while I question you about Nerita and your relationship with her."

Rex's hand dropped to his side and he gave me an angry look. "My relationship with Nerita is none of your business. It's a private matter. I'm not staying here to be asked questions about my private life." He turned on his heel and was about to march away.

I recalled Oliver's last words to me the previous day and decided it was time to be more assertive. I raised my hand and announced loudly, "Enough. I'll decide what's relevant to my investigation, not you."

I sent magic to my hands and aimed them at Rex. To my amazement, I managed to raise Rex and guide him back towards the chair he'd just vacated. It was like moving a man-sized balloon. I lowered my hand which made Rex settle into the chair. Continuing to use my magic, I immobilized his body beneath his head.

"What have you done to me?" he shouted. "Why can't you witches leave me alone? I've done nothing wrong."

I walked closer to him and folded my arms. My voice was calm as I said, "I want to know about your relationship with Nerita. When did it start? How long did it last? Who ended the relationship, and why? Rex, I'm not asking you this to be nosy, but I'm dealing with a murder investigation, and for all I know, you could have been the one who killed Nerita. You're not leaving this café until you've answered every one of my questions." I gave him a stern look to let him know how serious I was. Stanley came to my side and he glowered at Rex to show him how serious he was too.

Rex let out a sigh and said, "Alright, I'll tell you everything. Nerita and I had been a couple for a few years and we were getting along very well. She didn't want anyone to know about our relationship, especially not her father. Mermaids are not supposed to mix with other creatures in a romantic way. We both knew this, but we couldn't deny the attraction between us."

From his seated position, Jeremy said, "A doomed relationship. It's a tragedy waiting to happen."

Rex continued, "Things became serious between us. I proposed to her a few months ago and she said yes." A ghost of a smile flickered across his face. "But a few weeks after that, she changed her mind. She said she didn't have time to have a normal life like the other merpeople. She said she had to concentrate on being a leader especially now that her father was getting older. I told her I understood about her responsibilities and that I would support her. She said it wouldn't be fair to me if we married because she'd never be able to give me the full attention that I deserved." He lowered his head. "She said it was for the best that we separated. There was nothing I could do to change her mind."

"That's so sad," Jeremy said. "Did you kill her because she wouldn't marry you?"

Rex's head shot up. "Kill her? Why are you asking me that? I didn't kill Nerita. I loved her; I still do."

Jeremy stood up and reached into his pocket. He pulled out a notebook and handed it to me. "This is one of your mum's notebooks. She's got some comments in it about Rex and his terrible temper. He's caused many fights in his time."

"That was years ago!" Rex boomed. "Those fights happened when I was young and foolish."

Jeremy tapped the front cover of the notebook. "That's not all your mum wrote about Rex. There's a secret way into your world and Rex knows where it is. Your mum told him about it years ago in case he needed to go there in an emergency."

I narrowed my eyes at Rex. "Is this true?"

Rex nodded. "It's an underwater passageway. I've been through it a few times with Rosalyn."

"Did you tell Nerita about this secret passageway?" I asked.

"I did. As soon as I did so, I realised it was a mistake and I told her not to tell anyone."

I went on, "Does anyone else know about the passageway?"

"Not that I'm aware of." He hesitated and looked towards the sea. "That's not true. I suspect the sirens might know about it. I've been searching for them for days and can't find them anywhere. The only explanation is that they've gone into your world." He looked back at me and continued, "Before Nerita ended our relationship, she told me about the black cloud that had been hovering over the sea a month ago. The cloud turned into rain and it fell into the ocean in one particular area. Nerita went to that area and discovered that the black rain had turned into a small, black rock."

"What did she do with the rock?" I asked.

"Nerita told me she'd put it somewhere far away from Brimstone so that we'd be safe from whatever evil power lurked inside it. I fear she may have used the secret passageway and taken the rock into your world, Cassia. I don't know why she would do such a thing, but it seems the only explanation."

I looked down at Stanley and said, "What do you think about that? Does it make sense?"

Stanley said, "If Nerita put that rock in our world, what's going to happen to it there? And why have the sirens gone there too?"

I said to Rex, "Where does the secret passageway lead?"

"It leads to an area called Knotty Cove. I believe you used to visit that area with your mum and Gran."

I took a small step back in surprise. "Knotty Cove? Are you sure about that?"

Rex nodded.

I explained, "I used to go there with Gran after Mum passed away. We always had a marvellous time. It's a lovely place. Why would Nerita take that rock to Knotty Cove? Where did she put it?"

Stanley added, "And why did she order the sirens to go there too? Cassia, I don't like the sound of this at all."

"Me neither," I told him. "We need to get to Knotty Cove as soon as possible and find that rock."

Rex said, "I can take you there on my back. It's the quickest way to get there. We'll travel beneath the waves."

I waved one hand at him and removed the immobilising spell. I said, "Ok, let's do this straight away. I can use magic to allow me to breathe underwater. Stanley, you stay here with Jeremy."

Stanley puffed his little grey chest out and said, "No way. I'm coming with you. You can use the underwater spell on me too."

Chapter 25

Stanley refused to change his mind about coming with me and said in a brave voice, "I'll meet you at the water's edge. Can we be quick about this before I change my mind, please?"

He trotted out of the café and I had no option but to go after him.

Rex strode past me with his long, muscular legs and ordered, "Follow me."

Jeremy jogged at my side and said, "I'm not sure about Stanley going with you. Do you think he'll be alright?"

"I hope so. He's a stubborn little thing. I'll use that underwater spell on him and make sure it works before we set off. Jeremy, is it possible to use it all over Stanley so that his fur doesn't get wet? He hates it when his fur gets wet."

"Yes, we can do that." He quickly told me the words to use. "Do you want me to come with you? I've never been to that part of your world before and I'd love to see it."

I gave him a swift smile as I remembered the happy times I'd had at Knotty Cove. I said, "It's not a big town but the people there are very welcoming and friendly. It used to be a fishing village a long time ago, but when the fishing trade died out the people decided to do something else to ensure money still came into the community. There's a fishing museum there now and an aquarium. I've been to both of them many times with Gran and we always make a donation. They also run workshops on knot making." I stopped talking to see what Jeremy's reaction was to that piece of information.

"Knot making? Like a reef knot? And a rolling hitch? That sort of thing?"

"I don't know the names of the knots, but yes, those kinds of knots. In fact, Knotty Cove is a nickname that the residents came up with years back to increase tourism.

They've even got a website and Facebook pages. I can't see the fascination myself with knots, but some people seem to like it."

Jeremy stared into the distance. "I love knots and all the different varieties you can get. I've got a book on them. That workshop sounds amazing. How often do they have classes? Do you think I could enrol in one of them?"

I smiled at him as we walked along. "I'm sure something can be arranged. I'll sort it out for you after this investigation."

"Thank you," Jeremy said, with a huge smile on his face.

We came to a stop at the water's edge. Stanley was standing as close as he dared. He was giving the water a suspicious look and his whiskers were twitching in an irritated manner as if the water was offending him.

I said to him, "You don't have to come with me. You can stay here with Jeremy and tell him about the comb business."

Stanley lifted his little chin and said, "I've made my mind up. I'm coming with you. I trust your spell-casting abilities and know that no harm will come to me."

I was touched by his faith in me and hoped I wouldn't let him down.

Jeremy said, "What's all this about a comb? I thought that got sorted out."

I reached into my pocket and retrieved the hair comb. I told Jeremy where I'd found it as I handed it over to him. I said, "Could you talk to Isla about this? I think it's hers."

Jeremy's nostrils flared in anger. "Someone has been inside the lighthouse when you've been asleep? I definitely closed the door on my way out and I used magic to lock it." His nostrils flared again and his hand tightened around the comb. "I can't believe someone did that! Wait till I get my hands on them."

I placed my hand on his arm in an effort to calm him down. "I don't think whoever left it there meant us any harm. They're leaving us a message of some sort. Would you be able to look into this, please?"

Through gritted teeth, Jeremy said, "Yes, I'll deal with it alright. I'll find out who's been sneaking into the lighthouse in the middle of the night."

During my conversation with Jeremy, I hadn't notice Rex turning into his horse form. As impressive as he was in human form, he was magnificent as a horse. His white mane caught the wind and billowed behind him like a sheet on a washing line.

He turned his black eyes my way and said, "Are you ready? You'll have to climb onto my back."

Beads of sweat broke out on my forehead. I whispered to Jeremy, "How do I get on his back? He's enormous. Should I magic up a pair of ladders? I've never ridden on a horse before. What do I do? What do I hold onto?"

Jeremy replied, "Stop panicking. I'll help you onto his back. Your mum was just the same when it came to riding a horse. She conjured up a saddle so that she had something to hold onto. I remember the spell she used. Would you like me to use it now? I could even add a seat belt to keep you firmly in place. I think you'll need it; I've seen how fast Rex goes."

Stanley padded over to us and said, "I heard you saying something about a seatbelt. Can I have one too, please?"

Jeremy put the comb in his pocket and then waded through the water and over to Rex. He said to something to Rex before raising his hands at his back. Tiny, green sparks shot from his hands and landed on Rex's back. A brown saddle appeared there and I was pleased to see there were two seat belts on it; a large one for me, and a smaller one for Stanley.

Jeremy beckoned us over and then clasped his hands together and told me to put my foot into them. My legs shook as I did so and I thought there was no way Jeremy was going to be able to lift to me. He was going to cause damage to his back if he wasn't careful.

Jeremy made a low grunting noise as he heaved me onto Rex's back. I saw him wincing in pain as he did so and I could have sworn I heard something crack. Jeremy placed Stanley in my arms and I secured the little seatbelt around him. My hands were trembling as I fastened my own seat belt. Was it normal to be so high up on a horse?

Jeremy gave my leg a reassuring pat and said, "You'll be fine. I'm almost sure of it. Enjoy your trip."

My voice was too scared to come out so I gave him a swift nod and then gave Stanley a quick stroke of his head. It was more to comfort me than Stanley.

Stanley looked over his shoulder. "Cassia, you haven't done the underwater spell on us yet! Don't forget that!"

I took a steadying breath and then began to chant the spell. The only way of knowing whether or not it had worked was to go into the water.

I said to Rex, "Can you take us under the water slowly? I want to make sure my spell is working correctly."

"Of course, let's go." Rex took a few steps further into the sea.

I put my hand on Stanley's side and could feel his heartbeat going at an alarming rate. He was being so brave.

Rex cautiously moved further into the water until the sea flowed over his back. Stanley stiffened as water trickled over his paws. After a few more of Rex's steps, the water reached his chin.

Stanley said, "Cassia, I can't feel the water on me at all! I can see it going all over me, but I can't feel it. You spell is working."

I let out a sigh of relief and told Rex to go fully into the water.

He did so, and I was pleased to see Stanley breathing normally as we became submerged. I even heard him chuckle to himself. He was enjoying this.

Rex called out, "Are you ready to travel at speed now? Hold on tight."

Without any further warning, Rex took off running through the water at an impossible speed. It reminded me of being on an aeroplane when it suddenly speeds up and you leave your stomach five hundred yards behind you. The sea creatures around me became flashes of colour as we shot through the water.

In front of me, Stanley whooped with delight and raised his paws in the air. He called out, "Whoo! Yay! Go faster!"

I shook my head at my brave little cat. I wish I felt as brave. I was not enjoying this trip at all. It called to mind a horrible rollercoaster ride I'd been on once. It had gone up and down, back to front and even upside down. I'd been sick for hours afterwards. I decided the best course of action now was to close my eyes. I instantly felt better even though I was buffeted from side to side as Rex charged onwards.

Rex began to slow down after a few minutes and Stanley's shouts of joy began to subside. I opened my eyes and was surprised to see we'd arrived at Knotty Cove. Rex carried us out of the water and along the sand.

Rex said, "I'll drop you over at the side here where no one can see us. It wouldn't do for the humans to see me in this form."

He took us a short way down the beach and lowered himself so that I could climb off his back. I got off first and then reached for Stanley.

Stanley's mouth was pulled back in a smile and his eyes were wide with excitement. "Can we do that again? I want to do it again right now." He turned to Rex. "Thank you. That was amazing. So amazing. When can we do it again?"

Rex replied, "We can do it again when I take you back to Brimstone." He shook his mane and then turned back into his man form. He pointed ahead of us. "The sirens are here. I can see them. They're mixing with the humans. They shouldn't be doing that."

I looked towards the cove and the promenade at the top of it. Houses and shops lined the promenade and I recognised every building. Outdoor tables and chairs were occupied by the residents of the town. I knew them all. But I didn't know the long-haired women who were sitting with the residents and talking to them. Each woman was wearing a long, blue dress and they were barefoot. Unease grew in my stomach as I noticed the residents staring silently at the woman as if mesmerized. A slight humming noise drifted over to us and I realised that the women were now singing.

I said to Rex, Those women in the blue dresses, are those sirens?"

He gave me a tight-lipped nod.

"They look as if they're hypnotising people. Is that what they're doing?"

Rex couldn't hide the worry in his voice as he said, "That's exactly what they're doing. And they do that just before they lure humans to their deaths."

Chapter 26

I stared in horror at the scene in front of me. Normally, the people of Knotty Cove would be working in the shops and cafés or walking along the beach. The sight of them sitting silently in front of the singing sirens was sending chills racing down my spine. It was like watching a horror film when you know something awful is going to happen and all you can do is gawp at the screen.

I gave myself a mental shake and said, "I have to stop this immediately. Come on Stanley."

Stanley didn't reply and when I looked down at him, I saw a glazed expression on his face. He was moving from side to side as if listening to a song.

Rex explained, "He's under the sirens' spell. He must be able to hear their songs from here. The sirens will affect you soon."

"Not if I can help it." I quickly recalled all the spells I knew and thought a protective spell would be the best one to use. Magic rushed to my fingers and I moved them quickly over myself while reciting the spell's words. I did the same to Stanley and he immediately came out of his trance.

He gave me a confused look. "What happened to me? Did I fall asleep?"

"Almost."

Rex's jaw was hanging open and he now had a glazed expression on his face. I swiftly used my magic on him. His mouth snapped shut and he gave me a surprised look.

I told Rex about the spell I'd used. He said, "How long will it last?"

"I'm not sure, but I don't think we should hang around here for too long. Is there one siren in particular who's in charge? I want to find out why they are here and what they're going to do to the people."

Rex pointed to a lone siren who was sitting on a low wall to the right of the promenade. She had her attention on the rest of the sirens who were now singing even louder.

Rex said, "That's Ollyanne. She's the one in charge. Cassia, be careful around her. I've never heard her sing, but I've been told her mournful wails can make a creature lose their minds in a second. Do you want me to come with you?"

I didn't want to take the chance of Rex coming to any harm so I said, "No, thank you. You stay here. We'll be as quick as we can."

With Stanley in my arms, I hurried up the empty beach and over to Ollyanne.

Ollyanne's head turned our way as we approached and anger flashed in her eyes. Her long hair reached to her waist and it moved slowly from side to side as if it had a life of its own. She was wearing a long blue dress and was barefooted just like the rest of the sirens.

There was spite in her voice as she spat, "Cassia Winter, what do you want? You shouldn't be here. Clear off back to Brimstone."

I wasn't going to stand for any nonsense today. I replied curtly, "It's you and your friends who shouldn't be here. This is my world, and these are my people. Tell me why you and the other sirens are here. What are you intending to do to these people?" I sat next to her on the wall and looked directly into her eyes. "I don't want any lies. If I have to, I will use my magic on you."

Ollyanne looked me over. "You can't use your magic here. You'll get into trouble with Blythe if you use magic in this world. I know the rules."

"Blythe isn't in Brimstone at the moment, so I'm in charge. Which means I can use all the magic I wish to here. Why are you here?"

Ollyanne folded her arms and looked away, her hair flicked from side to side as if annoyed by my presence. "I can't tell you. I've been sworn to secrecy by Nerita. We're waiting for her further orders. She said she'd be in touch soon."

Stanley looked up at me and said quietly, "She doesn't know about Nerita."

Ollyanne turned her face back to us. "What did your cat just say about Nerita?"

I said in a gentler tone, "I'm sorry to tell you this, but Nerita is dead."

Ollyanne's hair stopped moving. She said, "Dead? She can't be dead. We're waiting for her orders. You're lying."

"I'm not lying. I'm investigating Nerita's death. That's why I'm here. My investigations have led me to you and this beach."

The siren shook her head in disbelief. "I don't understand. Why are you investigating her death?" She became still and comprehension dawned on her face. "She was murdered, wasn't she? Why else would you be investigating her death? Who killed her?"

"That's what I'm trying to find out. I suspect her death has something to do with you and the other sirens. I need an explanation from you. It's important."

Ollyanne pressed her lips together as if considering the matter.

My patience was running out. I said, "If you are here to cause harm to these humans, then I will stop you by whatever means I can. If Nerita asked you to hurt them for some reason, I have to know what that reason is."

Ollyanne gave me a slow nod. "I'm going to tell you the truth now. I don't know why we are here. Nerita brought us here and told us to get friendly with the humans so that they'd trust us. We're not here to cause them harm, I promise."

I frowned. "Why do they need to trust you?"

"Nerita said something terrible is going to happen in this area very soon; it's something to do with the seabed moving. When that happens, we have to lead the humans to safety. They will come with us quickly if they trust us.

That's why the other sirens are singing to them now. They're gently hypnotising them so that when the terrible event occurs, they will follow us immediately as we take them away from the danger."

I stiffened and remembered that Syloe had said something similar. "What do you mean about the seabed moving? What's going to happen here? And when is it going to happen?"

Ollyanne shook her head. "I don't know. I'm waiting to hear from Nerita about that. That's not going to happen now." She turned her head and looked towards the sea. "I can feel a change in the water out there. Something isn't right. Can you feel it too?"

Turning my head, I studied the water and noticed how calm it looked.

Stanley raised his paw and said, "Cassia, look at the horizon. The water looks peculiar. It looks like water boiling in a pan. Can you see it?"

I narrowed my eyes and focused on the horizon. Stanley was right. The sea there was moving in an unusual way and I saw water shooting up in several areas like geysers.

"You should speak to Nerita's uncle about the seabed," Ollyanne said. "When she first ordered us to come here, I asked her why. She said her uncle advised her to do so before the seabed moved. He'd told her that the humans here were going to be in peril when that happened and we had to protect them. She wouldn't give me any more details."

"Her uncle?" I looked down at Stanley. "I knew Mortimer was keeping something from us."

Stanley nodded. "We'll have to speak to him urgently."

I stood up with Stanley in my arms and said to Ollyanne, "You stay here with the others. As soon as you suspect danger is imminent, get these people to safety."

She nodded. "We will. Are you coming back?"

"Yes. I'd like to prevent the terrible event from occurring in the first place, if I can. I can only do that once I know what's going on."

I hurried down the beach and towards Rex.

Stanley shivered. "Did you hear that? It was like the sound of thunder. But it's coming from the sea."

I glanced towards the horizon again and noticed it was becoming more turbulent. I swallowed down my nervousness and broke into a run.

Rex must have picked up on my urgency because he immediately turned into his horse form and lowered himself. I jumped onto his back, secured us in place and told Rex to take us back to Brimstone as quickly as possible.

Before we were fully submerged in the water, I looked back at the lovely town of Knotty Cove and the wonderful people who lived there. I couldn't let anything terrible happen to them.

Chapter 27

Rex sped through the water and had us back at Brimstone Beach in next to no time. Stanley and I leapt off his back and ran along the sand. I'd left my broomstick in the café and I needed it urgently.

Jeremy was sitting on a blanket a short distance away and when he saw us, he got to his feet and waved the hair comb in the air. "Cassia, I've got something important to tell you about this comb."

I ran over to him and gasped, "There's no time for that. Knotty Cove and its inhabitants are in danger. We found the sirens. Nerita ordered them to go there to protect the humans because something terrible is going to happen soon." I ran out of breath and stopped speaking.

Stanley took over the explanation. "There's something wrong with the seabed in Knotty Cove. The sea doesn't look right and there's a weird noise coming from it. Nerita's Uncle Mortimer knows what's wrong with it, and we need to talk to him immediately."

I wheezed, "We need my broomstick. Just give me one more second to catch my breath."

Jeremy shoved the hair comb in his pocket and said, "There are other ways of travelling beside using a broomstick." He put his hands on my shoulders. "Can you conjure up an image of where Mortimer lives? I need you to be as clear as possible about the location."

"Why?" I asked.

"Because I'm going pick up on your thoughts and teleport us there."

Stanley punched his paw in the air. "Teleport us there? Wowsers!"

I picked Stanley up, closed my eyes and thought carefully about where Mortimer's dilapidated cottage was. Jeremy's hands on my shoulders felt heavy and my ears suddenly popped.

Jeremy moved his hands and said, "We're here."

I opened my eyes to find we were standing outside Mortimer's home. I mumbled, "How? What happened? How did you do that?"

Jeremy replied, "You have to be an extremely qualified witch to do that spell correctly. I'm sure Blythe or Esther will teach you how to do it in the future."

Stanley chuckled to himself in my arms. "Wow. I feel like I'm in a science fiction movie."

We walked towards the cottage and I rapped on the rotting wooden door. There was no answer but I heard a shuffling noise inside so I opened the door and stepped in.

I was expecting to find filth and ruin inside, but it wasn't like that at all. Everything sparkled and shone. The furniture was new and the decorations were tasteful and expensive-looking. There was an office area to one side and Mortimer was sitting there with his back facing us. Huge headphones covered his ears as he tapped away at a computer in front of him.

Stanley said, "Look at this place. It looks nothing like the outside. The outside is a disguise! That's so clever."

I didn't have time to be amazed by the scene in front of me. I put Stanley down, marched over to Mortimer and tapped him sharply on the shoulder. He jumped in surprise, spun around on his chair and removed the headphones. He was clean shaven and not wearing a disguise of any sort.

"What are you doing here?" he asked. "How did you get in?"

"Through the door. I want to know what's going on at Knotty Cove. What's wrong with the seabed?"

Mortimer blinked in surprise. "How do you know about that? Who told you? Whatever you've heard, it's all a lie. I had nothing to do with that black rock that was taken to Knotty Cove." He abruptly stopped talking and his glance slid to one side.

"No more lies! I know Nerita took a black rock into Knotty Cove. Where did she put it? On the seabed? Is that going to be the cause of the damage there? When will the damage occur? How bad will it be? If you tell me any more lies, I'm going to take strong action against you."

Mortimer rolled his chair back a fraction. "Nerita told me about the black rock she'd found in the Brimstone waters. It had come from that black cloud that had been hanging about. She knew the rock was dangerous and, in a panic, she went through the secret passageway to your world and planted the rock in the seabed there. She must have felt guilty because she confessed to me later about what she'd done." He pointed to the computer screen in front of him. "Despite not being allowed in the sea, I've kept up with what's going on there. I've been monitoring the flow and ebb of the sea in Brimstone in case anything untoward happens. When I heard about that black cloud appearing, I increased my surveillance."

I looked at the screen and couldn't make any sense of the swirls and numbers on it. I asked, "Where did you get this computer from?"

"Seeing as I'm mostly human now, it's easy for me to travel into your world. I love going there and getting equipment to help me with my inventions. When Nerita told me what she'd done, I went to Knotty Cove and set up some instruments there to measure unusual activity." He gave me a grim smile. "I soon found some. Nerita told me where she'd placed the rock and I placed underwater cameras there. Over the next few weeks, tentacles came out of the rock and reached out into the surrounding area. It was like the rock was alive. My equipment picked up on tremors and movement across that area. Those tremors have increased significantly in the last few weeks."

My legs felt wobbly and I lowered myself onto the table. "What's going to happen?"

"There's going to be a massive underwater earthquake very soon. It'll cause a tsunami which will destroy everything in its path. The authorities in your world don't know this is going to happen because the black force is invisible to them. I told Nerita this and that's why she ordered the sirens to go there. She needed time to work out how to remove the rock. She'd tried to do it herself, but the rock wouldn't budge. I offered my assistance, but she said it was her mess and she had to sort it out."

"Can we move the rock? Can I use magic on it?" I asked.

Mortimer shook his head. "It's too late. The tsunami will happen in the next few hours."

I jumped up. "Why didn't you tell me that immediately?" Rage coursed through me. "And why didn't you tell me any of this when we spoke before? I could have done something then."

Mortimer had the decency to look ashamed. "I didn't want to get involved in Nerita's business. I have nothing to do with the merpeople anymore."

I swallowed down my anger and said to him, "What can we do about this now? We can't let innocent people die."

Mortimer ran a hand over the back of his neck. "There's nothing you can do about the tsunami. However, you can get the sirens out of there before it's too late."

"Too late for what?"

He pointed to the screen. "The moving seabed is causing damage to the underwater passage. The sirens won't be able to use that soon. They'll be stuck in Knotty Cove forever. Even if they survive the tsunami, they won't thrive in your world. They'll probably die."

"There must be something we can do." I stared at the computer screen in horror hoping that it would give me an answer.

Mortimer said, "You can't save the humans, but you can save the sirens. If you go back now, you can order them to leave before the passageway is destroyed."

I continued to stare at the screen in hopelessness. A gentle breeze wafted against my cheek and I caught the slightest aroma of rose perfume. It was Mum's perfume. I closed my eyes and a feeling of calm slowly descended on me. An idea came to me. I knew without a doubt that if Mum were here, she'd agree with the course of action that was forming in my mind.

I turned to Jeremy and said, "I know what to do. I'm going to need your help."

Chapter 28

Jeremy shook his head vehemently when I told him my plan. "No! Absolutely not! It's dangerous. You'll kill yourself. I won't let you do it."

"You can't stop me," I told him. "I've seen the spell for calming the seas in one of Gran's books. I can't remember the words, but you must know them. Tell me what they are."

Jeremy folded his arms tightly over his embroidered waistcoat. "That spell is to calm turbulent seas in a storm. It'll be no use against a tsunami. Especially not one that's been caused by black magic!"

"But it might help lessen the damage," I argued. "Please, Jeremy, I have to try something."

His brow furrowed and he tightened his arms even more. "I won't let you do this. Your gran wouldn't want you to do this, and I know your mum wouldn't have."

I gave him a soft smile. "That's where you're wrong. I can feel Mum's presence. I can smell her perfume. Can't you?"

Jeremy's nose twitched and a look of surprise came over his face. His voice was less sure now. "This is a ridiculous plan."

"But it's the only plan we have. I have to try. Tell me the words to the spell."

Jeremy's arms dropped and he let out a dramatic sigh. "You are so stubborn. I will tell you the words, but only when we're at Knotty Cove. I'm coming with you."

"Me too!" Stanley announced. "I'll do what I can to help."

I lifted Stanley up and looked at his dear little face. I had no intention of putting him in harm's way.

"Stanley, I love you so much. I don't think I tell you that enough. You are my best friend." I smiled at him and stroked his head.

Stanley let out a little yawn. "I know you love me. Why are you telling me this now?" He yawned again. "Why are you looking at me like that?"

"Like what?"

"As if you'll never see me again." His eyes narrowed. "Are you casting a spell on me? Your hand feels suspiciously warm." He yawned again and his eyes began to close. His voice became drowsy. "Stop it, Cassia, stop making me tired. I want to come with you. I don't want to fall asleep."

As soon as his eyes closed completely, I put him in Mortimer's arms and said, "Take him to Gia at the beach café. Tell her I'll be back for him as soon as I can." I hesitated. "If I don't come back, tell her to take Stanley to Gran's house."

Mortimer frowned. "I haven't had anything to do with the creatures at Brimstone Beach for years. I'm not comfortable with talking to them."

"I don't care if you're comfortable or not. You should have told me about the black rock before. Taking Stanley to the café is the least you can do for me now. While you're there, speak to your brother and find out if he knew about Nerita taking the black rock to Knotty Cove."

"I'm not sure about that." Mortimer shifted in his seat.

I glared at him. "That was not a request. If King Taron doesn't know about the black rock, see if anyone else knew about it. Mortimer, the damage that's about to occur in Knotty Cove could have been prevented by you. As soon as you knew what Nerita had done, you should have informed me or another witch. We might not be facing this catastrophe now."

Mortimer wilted under my stare. "Okay, I'll do those things."

"Good." I gave him a tight smile. "Hopefully, I'll see you back at Brimstone Beach soon." I moved back to Jeremy. "Take us to Knotty Cove immediately."

Jeremy gripped my shoulders and green lights flashed all around me. A second later, we were standing on the sand at Knotty Cove. The sea roared in my ears and a strong wind whipped my hair across my face. The scene here had changed dramatically in the last thirty minutes.

Jeremy's face was aghast as he looked at the sea. "Look at it! It looks alive."

I took in the tumultuous water in front of me. It was rushing up the shore in anger and it looked almost black. I jumped out of the way as the water gushed over my shoes before it retreated with a low growling noise. Within two seconds, it rushed back and the water came to my knees knocking me backwards.

Jeremy caught me before I hit the sand. Above the noise, he yelled, "We have to move! The water's coming back even stronger." He dragged me away from the wall of water which was racing towards us like a wild animal.

I looked towards the row of buildings along the promenade and was shocked to see the residents standing there with horror on their faces. The sirens were clustered around them and appeared to be singing and pleading with the residents to move.

I called out to Jeremy, "The sirens' songs can't be heard above the noise!"

Jeremy gave me a grim nod. "Don't worry about the humans. I can deal with them. Order the sirens to return to Brimstone before it's too late." He dashed over to the nearest group of people and raised his hands. Sparks of green light shot from his fingers like shooting stars and landed gently on the people there. One by one, they hastened away.

I scanned the sirens' faces until I found Ollyanne. I raced over to her and shouted, "You have to take your sirens home right now! The passageway back won't last for much longer."

"But the humans," she started to argue with me.

"The humans are being dealt with. Go now! That's an order."

Ollyanne's face twisted with indecision.

I grabbed her shoulder and yelled again, "Go now! Before your way back has gone!"

Ollyanne nodded and within a minute, the bare footed sirens were running down the sand and into the churning sea. They dipped beneath the waves and soon disappeared.

"Please make it back safely," I muttered to myself.

Jeremy came to my side and shouted, "The humans are safe. I used a spell to make sure every resident knows they have to leave immediately." He turned to look at the sea. "It's time to perform our spell. I don't know if it will work, but it will be more effective if we say the words together."

The spray from the sea was now lashing at my face like a whip and I was finding it hard to speak. But I did my best to listen to the words that Jeremy was telling me. When I had them straight in my head, I said, "I usually try to keep calm when I'm performing a spell. I don't feel at all calm now; I feel sick to my stomach with worry."

Jeremy said, "This isn't the time for calmness or worry. This is a time for anger. The sea has turned into a furious beast, and we need to fight fury with fury." He raised his hands towards the sea. "Ready?"

It wasn't in my nature to be angry, but as I saw what the black magic was doing to this beautiful area, I felt an intense anger alight in my stomach. It flowed through my veins like fast moving lava. I'd never felt fury like it before.

I raised my hands and felt the familiar tingle in my fingers. The image of Astrid's mocking face came into my mind and the tingle increased. I muttered the words of the spell at the same time as Jeremy.

The faces of the creatures who had been murdered as a result of the evil magic appeared next to Astrid's face, and my fingers began to vibrate. Just like Jeremy, I repeated the words of the spell over and over again.

All the lovely beings in Brimstone, and now Knotty Cove, who'd been affected by the black magic dropped into my mind one by one. Blythe's face appeared, followed by Gran's and then Luca's. My anger increased with each image.

My hands were shaking by now and the words of the spell grew louder each time they left my mouth. I was oblivious to everything except the rage that had taken over my body and the words that I needed to say.

Still, the water continued with its attack as it lashed at us again and again. The water was up to my waist now and I was vaguely aware of things being knocked over behind me. My arms were throbbing with pain and it was getting harder and harder to keep them outstretched. I was drenched by this stage and my voice was hoarse. I was forced back as the water rushed at me. Somehow, I managed to stay upright.

With one last almighty effort, I screamed the words of the spell and roared with rage.

The sea water in front of me rose up and up like an animal standing on its hind legs, and, for a split second, it paused and there was a sudden silence.

Then the water crashed down on me forcing the breath from my body. I was flung backwards against something hard and pain exploded in my head. Everything around me went black.

Chapter 29

My eyes refused to open. They felt like they'd been glued together. I wriggled my fingers in an attempt to use magic to force my eyes open. There was no comforting tingle in my fingertips, but I could feel wet sand beneath my hands.

I felt someone kiss my cheek and move my hair off my face. I tried to talk, but my mouth remained shut. Was I even awake?

The kiss came again and I heard words of comfort being muttered. I couldn't tell if it was a male or female voice speaking to me. A sharper voice spoke and said something about moving me quickly and needing to use magic on me.

I didn't like the sound of that, and once again, I tried to open my eyes and mouth.

A sensation of weightlessness came over me and I felt myself moving forwards. I could also feel someone's hands beneath my knees and on my back. Someone was carrying me somewhere and I couldn't do anything to stop them.

Sudden warmth flowed through my body and I stopped thinking altogether.

The next thing I was aware of was a rough tongue licking my cheek, and the feeling of something furry against my chin. I recognised those sensations.

"Cassia! Wake up!" Stanley licked my cheek some more.

I opened my eyes without any trouble and saw Stanley's face inches away from mine. I reached out to stroke his little head and grimaced as pain shot through my aching arms.

"Hey there," I muttered to Stanley. "How are you?"

"Never mind me, what about you? You look like you've been in the wars. You've got bruises on your face and your clothes are torn." He nuzzled his head into my neck. "I've been worried sick about you. What happened?"

I raised my head and looked around me. "Why am I lying on Brimstone Beach? I was in Knotty Cove a minute ago. Where's Jeremy?"

"I don't know, and I don't know how you got here. I've been watching out for you from the café. I turned away for a moment to talk to Gia, and when I looked back, there you were, lying on the sand in this dishevelled state. Are you hurt?"

I tried to move my arms and flinched as pain shot through me. "I think I've done something to my arms with all the magic I used. Who brought me back here? Someone must have."

"I didn't see anyone." Stanley rested his head against my cheek. His voice was hoarse as he said, "I didn't think you were coming back."

"Neither did I for a while." With pain shooting through my arms, I managed to get myself into a seated position. I looked towards the café and saw Gia floating over the sand towards us holding something in her hands.

There was a mixture of concern and relief on her face as she came closer. "Here, drink this." She handed me a glass of something blue. "I'm so relieved you're back in one piece. Stanley and I have been so worried about you." She pointed to the glass. "Drink that now."

I did as I was told and then handed the glass back to her. The pain in my arms lessened and a spark of energy ignited in me. I felt able to stand up. As I did so, there was a flash of green light at my side and Jeremy appeared.

He looked worse for wear and his face looked much older. His beautiful embroidered waistcoat had been torn and there were cuts on his hands. He wrapped his arms tightly around me. "You're safe," he mumbled, "you're safe."

I waited for Jeremy to release his grip on me and then I took a step back. "What happened in Knotty Cove? Is everything okay there?"

Jeremy nodded. "I examined the area. The sea has returned to normal, and only a small amount of physical damage has been caused to the town. I found the humans and spoke to them. I told them we were from a secret environmental agency and the danger to their town had now passed. I could tell most of them didn't believe so I used a small amount of magic on them." He shot me a brief smile. "Cassia, we did it. We saved the town. We nearly died in the process, but we saved the town. How did you get back here?"

"I don't know. I did feel someone carrying me, but I don't know who."

Jeremy said, "Someone must be looking out for you." He sighed and patted his waistcoat. "I'm afraid this is beyond repair. I don't even want to see what my face looks like. Despite feeling the need to sleep for a hundred years, our investigation isn't over. I'm going to find Mortimer and see if he's found out who else knew about the black rock of doom." His glance went to my left arm. "You've hurt yourself. Why is your arm dangling at your side like that? Is it broken?"

I attempted to raise my left arm, but it refused to move. "It's not broken, just very tired. I think I've used all my magic up."

"You haven't, but you need to recharge, so to speak," Jeremy said. "There are some wonderful restorative potions in the bathroom at the lighthouse. I insist that you go back there now and have a long soak in the bath with one of those potions. You're no use to anyone in your present state."

"But we need to find out who knew about Nerita and the black rock," I argued. "It's important. I've got a strong feeling that it's connected to her death."

"Yes, I know it's important," Jeremy argued back. "Which is why I'm going to find out who knew. Then I'll go to the lighthouse and let you know." He put his arms on my shoulders and turned me in the direction of the lighthouse. "Off you go. Doesn't the thought of a warm bath sound appealing?"

I nodded.

Jeremy gave me a gentle push forward. "Stanley, you make sure Cassia has a long soak. I'll call on you both later."

Stanley replied, "I will do."

Stanley trotted dutifully at my side as we made our way to the lighthouse. I was worried for a second that I'd lost the key during my time fighting the sea at Knotty Cove, but thankfully, it was nestled safely at the bottom of my pocket.

Stanley stayed close to my side as we made our way up the spiral steps. I glanced at the lovely paintings on our left as we ascended. I hadn't had a good look at them yet. There were many images of the merpeople and showed scenes of their daily activities. I hesitated at one image and frowned at it. What did that mean? I looked at the next image which was slightly different. What was going on here?

Stanley nudged into my legs. "Keep moving. You're nearly there."

He kept bumping into my legs as he forced me up the stairs and towards the bathroom.

I looked down at him and said, "You've become very bossy, just like your brother."

He chuckled. "I know. Sometimes you have to be bossy." He cleared his throat and did a wonderful impression of Oliver. "Into the bathroom immediately, young lady! And don't come out until I tell you to!" He chuckled again.

I smiled down at him. "You are the best friend a witch could have. I won't be long in the bathroom."

"Take your time. I'll wait for you outside."

Once inside the bathroom, I switched the taps on and water gushed out at a pleasing speed. The tub would be filled in no time. I opened the bathroom cabinet and saw many glass bottles containing bubble bath potions. Each bottle had been labelled with a different ailment which could be cured:

'Sea serpent bites'

'Grindylow scratches and bruises'

'Squid ink poison'

'Tentacle trauma'

'Sand-snake rash'

My eyebrows rose. Most of the bottles had already been opened. What had Mum got up to during her time here? That's something I'd ask Jeremy later. I settled on a bottle labelled 'General aches and pains'. I poured a liberal amount into the tub and a relaxing aroma of lavender filled the air.

I peeled off my damp and damaged clothes and dropped them on the floor. I climbed into the welcoming tub and the restorative effects of the hot water and the lavender scented bubbles got to work on me instantly. The aches and pains melted from my arms completely and I was able to lift them easily.

I leant my head back and took a full minute to relax. I lifted my head back up and nodded to myself. That was enough relaxing. I had a murder investigation to deal with. My head felt clearer now and the images of the paintings I'd seen on the way up the stairs flashed into my mind. Why were they so important? Why were those particular images standing out to me?

Something shiny caught my attention on the floor. I looked that way and saw something poking out of my trouser pocket. It was something I hadn't put there. It was a hair comb. A shiny, hair comb that I'd seen before.

The bits of confused information came together in my head like a dreadful jigsaw.

I groaned and put my head in my bubble-covered hands.

It was starting to make sense now.

Chapter 30

I stayed in the bath a short while longer until I accepted the facts. I nodded to myself. Okay, I had to deal with this. And I had to deal with it now. Could this be related to Nerita's death? I wasn't sure I wanted to make that connection.

I got out of the bath and quickly dried myself. I wrapped Mum's dressing gown around me and the aroma of her perfume enveloped me like a reassuring hug.

I found Stanley sitting on Jeremy's knee on the sofa in the living area. Jeremy was wearing a different waistcoat and his face looked just as perfect as when I'd first met him.

"Oh! I wasn't expected to see you back here so soon," I said to Jeremy.

Stanley said, "And I wasn't expecting your bath time to end so quickly."

"I've been in there long enough. I feel much better now." I moved over to the sofa and sat next to Jeremy. "What have you found out?"

"Thanks to the helpful grindylows, I've discovered that King Taron refused to come to the surface to speak to Mortimer. Mortimer left the beach in a huff and returned home."

"That's a shame. I wanted to know if King Taron knew about Nerita taking the black rock to Knotty Cove."

Jeremy raised a finger. "Thanks again to the nosy grindylows, I now have some information on that. Shortly before she died, Nerita did tell someone about the black rock. She told them everything including the danger she'd put the humans in."

"Really? Who did she tell?"

Jeremy sighed. "The grindylows don't know. Nerita was on the beach and the being she was talking to was standing behind a rock. The grindylows did hear Nerita's voice rising as she tried to defend herself. Whoever she spoke to was furious about what she'd done and at the end of the conversation, she yelled, 'I wasn't thinking about the humans! I was concerned with my subjects here! They're more important.' She then stormed off and returned to the sea."

"What did she mean by those words? Didn't she care about the impending disaster that was going to occur in Knotty Cove?"

"I don't think she did. After I'd spoken to the grindylows, I appeared in Mortimer's cottage and spoke to him. When he returned home, he checked the monitoring equipment at Knotty Cove." Jeremy gave me a wide smile. "The black rock has gone. His graphs show that it disintegrated around the time we were performing our spell. He's going to keep an eye on that area and will let us know if anything peculiar turns up. That's one problem sorted out."

I gave him a nod and then reached into my pocket. I pulled out the hair comb that I'd picked up from the bathroom floor. "Look what I've found."

Jeremy's eyes widened. "Not again! Where did you find it? Has our devious intruder been at work again?"

"I think it might have been placed in my pocket when I was lying on the sand on Knotty Cove. I think the being who put it there brought me back home too." I handed the comb to Jeremy. "It's Isla's comb, isn't it?"

Jeremy lifted it to the light. "It is. But it doesn't belong to her anymore. Her engagement to Conway has been broken off. I tried to tell you that earlier, but we got caught up in the drama at Knotty Cove."

"Who broke it off?" I asked. I feared I already knew the answer.

Jeremy lowered the comb. "Conway did." He gave me a serious look before continuing. "Do you know what this means?"

"I think so. There are some paintings on the wall next to the stairs. They show mermen leaving hair combs in the homes of mermaids. Later on, the pictures show the couple getting married. I think that mermen leave combs in someone's home as a way of proposing. Am I right?"

Jeremy gave me a slow nod.

Stanley said, "I'm confused. Cassia, does this mean that someone has proposed to you?"

"I think so. I've found this comb three times now."

There was silence as we all digested this information.

Stanley said, "Does that mean Conway has proposed to you? You hardly know him. The cheek of him! Don't accept his proposal. You can't live in the sea with him. You'll go all wrinkly!" His voice rose in panic.

"I've no intention of accepting his proposal. I had no idea he had feelings for me. I'll speak to him and give him the comb back."

Jeremy picked Stanley up and placed him on my lap. "You're not going to talk to him. I will. Mermen can become aggressive when they don't get what they want. You stay here and I'll come back after I've spoken to Conway. I'd like to know how he got into your apartment and in here without a key!" He got to his feet. His face was scrunched up in annoyance.

"I can deal with this myself."

"Not in your dressing gown. I won't be long." Jeremy strode away and thudded down the stairs before I could argue with him.

I said to Stanley, "I should be the one who talks to Conway. I'll quickly get dressed and then we'll go after Jeremy. I spotted some of Mum's clothes in a drawer under the bed. I hope they fit me."

The clothes did fit me. The jeans were torn around the knees and there was a stain on the T-shirt, but that didn't matter. I even found a clean pair of socks at the back of the drawer.

As I pulled the socks on, Stanley cocked his head to one side and said, "Did you hear that? There's someone upstairs on the balcony. I'm going to have a look." He scampered off.

"Stanley! Wait!" I ran after him, my socks slipping on the wooden floor. "Stanley, don't go up there without me!"

I raced up the stairs and noticed the door at the top was open. I went out onto the balcony and came to a sudden stop.

Conway was standing a few feet ahead of me. Stanley was in his arms and was struggling to get free.

"Cassia! There you are. We've got a lot to talk about, haven't we? We've got plans to make and things to discuss. Now that Nerita is out of the way, you can become my queen." He smiled broadly as if he were delivering the best news ever.

I gripped the wooden rail at my side for support. "Conway, did you kill Nerita?"

His eyes twinkled with joy. "Of course I did. I did it for you, my love."

Chapter 31

My knees felt weak and my grip on the handrail increased.

"What do you mean?" I asked. My glance kept going to Stanley and I could see how much he was struggling to get out of Conway's arms.

Conway took a step closer. "I fell in love with you the second I saw you, Cassia. Then, when we went into the café and you had that ice cream which made you glow with happiness, my love intensified and I knew I'd do anything for you. I told you then I'd find out what had happened to the missing sirens, and that's what I did. I confronted Nerita and demanded that she tell me the truth. I've known for weeks that she was up to something." He shook his head sorrowfully. "She told me about that black rock of magic that she'd put in your world. In your world, Cassia! She said it was going to cause damage there and that humans could be killed. Your people, Cassia! She was going to hurt your people in your world. And she didn't care! I couldn't have that. I had to get rid of her." He laid a heavy hand on Stanley. "I did it for you and your world. Your old world, that is. You're going to be part of my world soon. To be honest, I've been thinking about doing away with her for a while. She was so rude to me and alway put me down in front of the other mermen."

I noticed Stanley had pulled one of his paws free. I played for time and said, "How did you do it? How did you kill her? How did you get that pure water into a bottle without hurting yourself?"

He gave me a lingering look. "I love how you're so concerned about me. It was Von who did it."

"Von?"

"Yes, the sea hag. She has magical abilities. Nerita used one of Von's magical potions when she went to see Uncle Mortimer in the forest." He smiled. "I knew about her secret visits to Uncle Mortimer. Isla told me. She was a nosy mermaid, but useful for a while. I ordered Von to fill that bottle for me. I also ordered Von to give me an enchanted key which would open any door. Von can't disobey me, not when I'm going to be king soon. You should meet her. You'll like her. She'll help you turn into a mermaid. She's already got the spell ready. Von's amazing. She even put a spell on me on the day I turned up at your apartment. Her spell made it appear that I was dying. You helped me. I knew you would. I could see the love in your eyes as you looked after me."

Stanley had another paw free.

I continued, "You put the comb in the apartment in town."

"I did. I prised it from Isla's fingers when I ended our engagement. She didn't take that news easily." He took another step forward. "You are so beautiful when you're asleep. I watched you for hours. Why did you give the comb back to Isla the next day?"

"I thought she was the one who left it in the apartment."

He nodded. "That's what I thought. I took it from Isla, yet again, and made it clear that our engagement was over. I ordered her to leave Brimstone. Then I came here and put the comb next to your bed downstairs when you were asleep." He squeezed Stanley's back. "I don't want this creature sharing a bed with you again. It's not fitting for a queen." He tilted his head. "But then you gave the comb to that stupid witch friend of yours. Why?"

Conway's hand was resting too heavily on Stanley's back and I could see him struggling to breathe. I forced a smile to my face and said, "I'm ignorant in the ways of the merpeople. I didn't know what it meant. Was it you who brought me back from Knotty Cove?" I remembered the kisses on my cheeks and tried not to shudder.

Conway said, "Of course it was me. I couldn't leave you in that dreadful place. Von helped me bring you back home." An annoyed look came into his eyes and he looked down at Stanley. "Keep still! Stop wriggling!"

I moved closer to Conway and held my arms out. "Give Stanley to me. I'll look after him." I attempted to send magic into my fingertips. As soon as Stanley was free, I was going to use an immobilising spell on Conway.

Conway's face twisted in disgust as he looked at Stanley again. "What do you need this creature for? It can't even swim. It's of no use to us."

Conway suddenly turned to the side and flung Stanley over the wooden rails. I froze and my heart stopped beating. Conway grabbed my outstretched arms and pulled me into his tight embrace. "It's just the two of us now."

"Nooooo!" I screamed. I wriggled in his arms. "Nooooo! Stanley! Let me go!"

Conway squeezed me so hard that I couldn't breathe. I couldn't move. I couldn't use my magic. I heard a distant yowl from Stanley and I went limp in his arms.

Stanley. My Stanley.

The ferocious rage that I'd felt at Knotty Cove awoke in me. In an instant, I pulled myself free and shot a dose of magic at Conway's smug face. I spun around and looked over the rails hoping to see Stanley somewhere. My fingers tingled ready to shoot magic out to save him somehow. Where was he? My vision blurred with tears. Stanley? Where are you?

I heard a meow behind me and turned around.

Luca was standing there. He had Stanley safely in his arms.

Stanley said, "Luca caught me! He saved my life."

I couldn't move. Love for Stanley welled up in my heart along with tears in my eyes. I gulped and said, "I thought I'd lost you."

Luca said briskly, "I was on my way over to see you when I saw your cat in the arms of a merman up here. I could sense that things weren't right so I stopped next to the wall and listened to what the merman was saying." He gently stroked Stanley's head and his tone softened. "I'm glad I was ready to catch this little fella. Are you okay, Stanley? That must have been quite a shock for you. I know you like flying on Cassia's broomstick, but this can't have been pleasant."

Stanley said, "How do you know I like flying?"

Luca frowned. "I don't know. I just do." He rubbed the back of his hand against Stanley's cheek. "And I know you like it when I do this."

Stanley purred.

Luca laughed and then looked over at Conway who was frozen in place. He said, "Who's he, and why did he throw Stanley over the rails? Are you two getting married?"

I wiped my tears away and walked over to him. "No, I'm not getting married. He killed his sister. I'll tell you about it in a minute." I held my hands out. "Can I have Stanley back, please? Thank you for saving him." Fresh tears rolled down my cheeks.

Luca put Stanley in my arms and then, to my surprise, he reached out and wiped my tears away with the back of his hand.

He pulled his hand back and stared at it in astonishment. "What's happening? Why is my hand glowing like that? What's in your tears? Magic?"

We watched as my tears stood out like diamonds on the back of his hand. They glowed silver and then turned into tiny stars. The stars grew bigger and floated towards Luca's head. They settled on his hair like a crown.

Stanley said to me, "Are you doing that?"

I shook my head. "I don't know what's happening to him."

The stars suddenly popped and vanished.

Luca blinked in surprise and then gave me a studied look. "Cassia? Cassia Winter? And you, Stanley." He blinked again. "I remember you; both of you. I remember everything."

Hope pierced my heart. "Everything? I said. "What do you mean by that?"

He smiled and his blue eyes sparkled with warmth. "Everything. All our time together as children, and our time together when you came back to Brimstone." His smile faltered. "I remember Astrid and what she did to me before she left. Oh! I've been awful to you. The things I've said! I'm so ashamed. Can you forgive me?"

"We already have," Stanley announced. "Do you really remember us? Are we friends again?"

Luca nodded. He placed his hand on my arm and said, "We'll always be friends. Cassia, don't ever let that happen to me again. If I lose my memories, do magic on me! Get all the witches in the land to do magic on me! I don't want to forget you ever again. Neither of you."

I smiled at him and my heart felt lighter than it had done in days, perhaps weeks. As I beamed at him like a fool, I recalled something he'd said a few minutes ago.

"You said you were on your way to see me? Why?"

"Your gran and Blythe have returned to Brimstone safe and well. They want to see you. They are too tired to come here themselves, so I offered to do so."

Fresh tears sprang from my eyes. "They're back? And they're safe?"

"They are. Come here." Luca put his arm around me and pulled me close. "There's no need to cry. Everything is okay now."

"I know," I mumbled into his chest. "These are happy tears."

Stanley sniffed in my arms. "Mine are happy tears too."

I let the tears ebb away and continued to rest my head against Luca's chest. I knew I had to deal with Conway soon, and I was anxious to see Gran and Blythe again. But, just for now, those things could wait. This was a lovely moment, and I wanted to enjoy it for as long as possible.

Luca sniffed and said, "You smell nice. You smell of roses."

I smiled and felt Mum's love wash over me. Just one more minute and then I'd return to my life as a justice witch.

One more minute. Maybe two.

About the author

I live in a county called Yorkshire, England with my family. This area is known for its paranormal activity and haunted dwellings. I love all things supernatural and think there is more to this life than can be seen with our eyes.

I hope you enjoyed this story. If you did, I'd love it if you could post a small review. Reviews really help authors to sell more books. Thank you!

This story has been checked for errors by myself and my team. If you spot anything we've missed, you can let us know by emailing us at: april@aprilfernsby.com

You can visit my website at: www.aprilfernsby.com

Sign up to my newsletter and I'll let you know how to get a free copy of my new books as I publish them. You can sign up on my website.

Many thanks to Paula for her proofreading work: https://paulaproofreader.wixsite.com/home

Warm wishes
April Fernsby

The Brimstone Witch Mysteries:

Book 1 - Murder Of A Werewolf

Book 2 - As Dead As A Vampire

Book 3 - The Centaur's Last Breath

Book 4 - The Sleeping Goblin

Book 5 - The Silent Banshee

Free short story - The Leprechaun's Last Trick

The Murdered Mermaid
A Brimstone Witch Mystery
(Book 6)
By
April Fernsby
www.aprilfernsby.com

24779669R00103

Printed in Poland
by Amazon Fulfillment
Poland Sp. z o.o., Wrocław